Covey Jencks
By
Shelton L. Williams

Southern Owl Publications, LLC
13607 Suite 100 Terrace Creek Drive, Louisville, KY 40245
www.southernowlpublications.net

Ordering Information:
Quantity sales. Special discounts are available on quantity purchases by corporations, associations, and others. For details, contact the publisher at the address above.

Printed in the United States of America

TABLE OF CONTENTS

Foreword

A decade or so ago, I stopped writing about international politics and started writing about murder and mayhem in the USA. The first two books I wrote were non-fiction and highly personal. Covey Jencks is fictional and also personal but not in the same ways as my first two. I care about the places, people, and events in *Covey Jencks,* but the circumstances and specifics of the story are the product of my imagination entirely. *Covey Jencks* includes persons of color, persons of different levels of education, and persons who are both cisgender and non-cisgender. The author is an old white guy and what we used to call straight, so what is he doing writing and talking about these other folks? I hope that he is trying to show that people are people and all of us are mixed in attitudes, assumptions, and experiences. It's the human condition. Thanks to my African-American, Hispanic, straight and gay, and young and old friends (of various hues and orientations) who proof-read the manuscript, commented on the language, and proffered advice on the story. I especially thank the readers from West Texas and from the Rotary Club of Washington, D.C. They are all rich in diversity and as earthy as they come, so their views helped me a lot. Everyone had colorful comments and I hope that you, dear reader, benefit from our collective effort. Any errors that remain are mine and mine alone.

Shelly

Cast of Characters

Covey Jencks, young lawyer who grew up in Odessa, TX

Frank-Covey's dad, car wash owner

Freddie Mae-worked at the car wash, victim

Wild Bill-Bill O'Toole, down from Boston, worked at the car wash

Jack-works at Jencks and Associates

M.A.-works at Jencks and Associates

Beth-M.A.'s friend

Erica-intern at Jencks and Associates

Alberto-young Associate at Jencks and Associates

Willie-Freddie's friend, tough guy

Cleon-Freddie's almost Ex

Rosa-works at the car wash

Gro-works at the car wash

Delbert and Aaron Carleton-almost rich rancher "boys"

Dan and Bo Gladstone-Covey's "friends" from childhood, now grown up

Bradley Harper-Front Desk clerk

Callie-Covey's high school girlfriend

JayJay-AKA Bonnie Jay., B.J., and J.

China-Pronounced Cheena, works in Juarez for Hector

Larraine-businesswoman on the south side

Thomas Franklin, owner, Ranger Hauling, Abilene, TX

Chapter 1
Home Again

I never intended to come back to West Texas. It's hot and dusty, yes, but that's not the thing. I like hot, and dusty is usually temporary. I don't even mind the tornado warnings. Like all West Texans, I am just happy not to live where there are earthquakes or subways. Getting in my jeep and driving wherever the hell I want at whatever the hell speed I want is freedom to me. I like freedom. It's why I am not married. It's why I almost never wear a suit. It's why, despite my long-standing misgivings and intentions, I am in Odessa, Texas and not in Washington, D.C.

OK, let's back up. Yes, I could be in D.C. In fact, I was there once, and I mean actually living there, for about nine months. I never got an apartment and I never set down roots, but I was there. I was at the law firm of Stanley and Sachs at 18th and K St., NW, as an associate almost right out of law school and I lived at the Carlyle Suites hotel just off DuPont Circle in downtown D.C. Law review, law school contacts, great interviews and a successful clerkship got me a $100,000 first-year job upon finishing third in my class at UT Law. I deferred a year to clerk on the Fifth Circuit on New Orleans and make pretty good money there, too. I could afford Washington and, because it was Stanley, I went. I could afford D.C. life, but I hated it.

Let me be clear. I did love D.C. in many ways. Too much. The restaurants. The women. The City. Yes, I loved it, but I was not supposed to love it that much. I was supposed to focus on my job, my career. I was supposed to dress a certain way, to represent a company that I came to despise, and to pretend that I gave a shit. I was expected to become a Washington lawyer. Little did I know that being a lawyer was not nearly the same as becoming a lawyer. Besides, by the time I got to D.C., I was almost grown. I was already 31 when I arrived. I had delayed law school for four years in the Army (82nd Airborne) just before the First Persian Gulf War under the "good Bush." I had worked hard at UT Law and made my parents, Austin College in Sherman, TX, my small Liberal Arts College, and my girlfriend all very proud. Everyone said that I had a great future. I had done well, even coming from Odessa and even being a former football player. D.C. meant that I had made it. The sky was the limit.

How did I know that I would come to love D.C. social life so? How did I know that being an Associate at Stanley would be like being in the Army but without the charms of Basic Training? How did I know that after about two months, all my personal discipline, professionalism, and willingness to submit to authority would disappear? How did I know that I would one day suddenly realize that the sacrifices, self-denials, and self-deceptions I had endured would crash and burn like the Iraqi army on the Highway of Death on the road to Baghdad? What I did know pretty fast was that working for Stanley, unlike law school, football season, and basic training, did not have an end date that would eventually free me to be my real self, the self that emerged after leaving Odessa, going to the military, and surviving law school. A wise person once told me that staying in a job you hate is one of life's greatest regrets. I decided to get the hell out.

I guess any thinking person could have seen it coming. Eventually my girlfriend had given up on me. I stopped pretending to be West Texas religious in college and especially in Austin. Callie, I called her Callie Mae, came a step or two in my direction but would not, could not, go any further. She had tolerated visiting Austin, but she did not like it. She began to hate my attitude and my overly logical mind. I know what you're thinking. We "outgrew each other after I left college." No, or maybe yes, but the sordid truth is that even before that, I had sex with an Assistant Manager at Scholz's Beer Garden, thought for about thirty seconds I was in love with her, grew distant from the hometown sweetheart, and in reality, pushed away the girl I was "meant" to marry. Scholz's did not last, but the breakup did. I embraced the freedom.

But the Army was not for me and D.C. was not for me. Corporate law was not for me. I had been a good boy in high school, but a bit in college and a lot in the Army had stretched my appreciation of "good." My dorm, Luckett Hall, at Austin College had been full of smart, resourceful and marginalized guys who smoked dope, chased women and some men, and made good grades. They also pulled pranks and told tales that changed my whole world view, even as I studied a great deal more than any of those geniuses. Someday I may tell you about them, but for now, believe me. I saw a new way of livin' there and in four years in the army, three years of law school, one year in 'Nawlins, and 9 months in D.C. There was nothing close to what I really needed in D.C. Nothing was nearly enough.

13

But then, how could Odessa offer what I wanted? Granted one good thing was that my parents were no longer there. Callie Mae was no longer there. College and Teacher's Ed had taken her to Wichita Falls. My mother had died of congestive heart failure in my last year of law school. My dad, even though alive, was also dead to me. He was the dark force in my life that both drove me to academic excellence and showed me what limits there were to being an irresponsible asshole. In both cases I was driven to be absolutely nothing like him. It makes me nervous when I see reflections of him in my personality and I see those reflections everywhere, all the time. How can one have a family, be successful without selling your soul, actually help others, and act totally unencumbered? The answer? Don't get married; own your own business; and don't take on causes. And don't work for Stanley and Sachs.

But even work for anyone, anywhere? Despite the pay, it's not worth it. The Army taught me that. I survived because I was smart. I passed an intelligence test that got me into a management position at Fort Bragg, home of the 82nd Airborne. I was in Acquisitions, a necessary and important function that bored me to tears and made me resent officers who thought their education, rank, or hometown made them better than me. My West Texas masculinity was fully engaged, and I had my revenge not in the workplace but in screwing not one but two of their wives. All right. I apologize for my immature reaction to authority, but the ladies did not at all seem to mind. My girlfriend never knew, but she eventually drifted away.

I thought I would "grow up" in law school, in D.C., or sometime. Hasn't happened yet. So, I am going to live my life and try not to impose my freedoms on any woman or kids. I will also avoid married women. No more unhappy, hot women who married the wrong guy for the wrong reasons. D.C. or New York, see you down the line or never. I am back to West Texas where I can take my earnings from Stanley and an unexpected windfall from my dad, buy a small building on Lee St. in Odessa, and practice oil and gas law with folks who survived the most recent oil bust in West Texas. I will just never mention that Bill Clinton is all right with me. His politics, his appetites, and his policies are fine with me. There you have it. I am a mess. That, and I have unfinished business in Odessa, By God, Texas.

Chapter 2
The Day Freddie Died

The Odessa cops thought nothing of the dead hooker's body on the side of the road not too far from a decrepit old barn. Neither dead bodies nor whores were unusual in an oil boom town, even in 1979. The road where a truckload of roughnecks found her led to an oil lease south of Odessa on the Old Crane Highway. It was unpaved and litter-filled with random pieces of soiled paper, Minit Market packaging, and beer cans strewn around the body. The woman, black and somewhat hefty, was wearing a blue nightie; she had one gold tooth in front and a Jim Bowie knife deeply imbedded in her chest.

"I take it that whoever kilt her wasn't no nigger-lover," said Deputy Dan Gladstone when he first saw the body. Such was the level of insight and sophistication of Odessa in 1979. The *Odessa American* did not report the story and no one in white Odessa ever knew much about her murder. The police arrested, prosecuted, and incarcerated her almost ex-husband for the death and no one seemed to care about either him or her on either side of the tracks in Odessa. No one that is except me, Covey Jencks. The death of Freddie Mae Johnson turned my life upside down and initially sent me far away from deep West Texas. From the day she died, I sought a path out of oil country and its black gold, ultimately moving to a city of political power and the hope of a different life. I did not know Washington, D.C. but I believed that by going there someday I could change the rules of the game. I did not know how long a trip it would be, how different D.C. would be from my naive image, or that, seemingly, while I left Odessa, Odessa always followed me. Eventually not Odessa but Freddie Mae's death drew me back.

Chapter 3
Odessa Then

Freddie Mae died in March 1979, while I was a junior at Odessa Permian High School. You know, Friday Night Lights and all that. In fact, I played on the team, lettered in fact. I was not a stud, but I did have a reputation for covering kick offs. Our trainer, Doc Andersen, calculated that I was in on almost half of the tackles on kick offs that year. And we kicked off a lot. We were 8-2 that year, beating most teams by two touchdowns or more, but with two losses we did not even win district. Nevertheless, we were on the verge of something big as a team and as a school. Just the next year we would begin a long stretch of dominance and excellence that would result in being named the number one team in high school football in America in 1989 and the winningest team in all of Texas during that decade. ESPN, HG Bissinger, Hollywood, and NBC would cement our image as THE football school in America. Unfortunately, by 1980, when we won our third state championship, I was nowhere to be found on the football team. Freddie, work, and family took care of that.

Like my own father, for most Odessans education was something to be endured and only the hard knocks of life could teach you a damn thing. The sooner you learned that you had to do it yourself, the sooner you could make it in America. Daddy wanted me working, not wasting time playing ball or even studying. In his way Daddy was also ill suited for Odessa. He appreciated the rough and tumble of the oilfield but as a businessman, he was not in Rotary, the

Chamber of Commerce, and most importantly, not the Baptist Church. Daddy had his own creed for life and none of it fit polite society, in Odessa or anywhere else.

What actually passed for moral guidance in Odessa then and now were the teachings of fundamentalist Christianity. This was true in white churches and black but, in the latter, the prevailing message was God's forgiveness for sins and in the white churches the promise of the burning pits of hell awaited. A second message in white churches was the notion that American decline begun under F.D.R. had accelerated and now a Communist conspiracy had taken over in Washington. What did I know? What did I care? My family was neither religious nor political. As a kid, I just wanted to make a tackle or hit a baseball. As a teenager, I just wanted to get laid. But to my dad's lasting disgust I did want to make good grades. The grades were neither for the future nor for getting girls. They were for me. They were for being a good boy and for not being like my father. Teachers gave gold stars for good grades. You got your name in the paper for good grades. Getting all the answers right meant in some way you were, uh, better than others. As I grew up, I could not hit the curve well enough. The other boys excelled at football, got the girls, and played cards. They were men. My companions were Dickens, Albee, and Salinger. I didn't mean to be different. It just happened. After a while, I not only wanted good grades; I needed them. Grades were my biggest concern until Freddie died.

I had one other little obsession, one little secret-Sex. And to my shame how and where I pursued it I kept secret then and for many years in the future. My dad owned the car wash in Odessa and at the car wash he employed African-Americans and Mexican-Americans almost exclusively. These were the invisible people of Odessa and to a person everyone lived south of the tracks and could never be seen downtown or on the streets of Odessa after the sun went down. Unknown to my parents and to my white friends, the black folks at my dad's place became the center of my social life and the adults taught me to dance, drink beer, and when I wanted, actually enjoy church. Now, for the most part, they knew that the separation of white and black was the "normal" thing, but they also knew that other white men, including my daddy, sometimes came to the south side for less than religious reasons. My going over was innocent, at least at first, and a night at Fatman's BBQ was a lot more fun than a cotillion at the Odessa Country Club. Not that I ever got invited to the annual cotillion, but I saw the kids who went in their white sports' coats and light blue prom dresses and, well, I just figured. Still, I felt secretly ashamed that I had to go south to be appreciated and to try to fulfill my teenage obsession.

I not only kept Fatman's and the south side secret, but I also kept Bonnie Jay secret. B.J. was my age. She sometimes worked at Fatman's. She was a cheerleader at Ector High School, the mostly minority school in Odessa. And she was smart, funny, and sexy as hell. After a few visits south, we became friends and then slightly more than friends. A kiss here, a close dance there. Excitement always. That I liked her and that I kept her a secret was, of course, like my dad. Daddy always led two lives and one of those lives was on the south side and much of it involved Freddie Mae. Later it hit me that I, too, was racist. I, too, played at a double life. I, too, acted like only one side of my existence mattered. The funny thing was that B.J. was a totally upright citizen and I behaved towards her even more gentlemanly than I did towards Callie.

I finally broke it off with B.J. after six or eight months of seeing her at Fatman's and taking her on dates to Ben's Little Mexico on the south side. We talked a lot and made out a little. I think she really liked me, but I broke it off. I did not do it because she was black, not because she ever complained about not going downtown to the movies with me, not because I feared exposure of my secret life, but because B.J. did not put out. I mean, I never really tried with her, but I thought that it would just happen. Deep inside my racist soul I thought a black girl would have sex more easily than a white girl; she would have an easy virtue; she would solve my "problem." She would initiate it.

"Why did you go and break it off with that girl, Covey Jencks?"

Freddie Mae was cleaning the inside of a blue Ford Fairlane as I drove it from the vacuum to the steam cleaning station at the entry way to the car wash. We often grabbed conversation in 30 second trips from the vacuum to the steam pit. Usually a full conversation would take the better part of a morning, but this time no car was behind the Ford, so I did not get out when we reached the pit. With Freddie I was always totally honest-eventually.

"What did B.J. say?"

"She say you tole her it was over and you didn't give her no good reason. She say you acted real funny."

"Well, you know that I got another girl friend."

"Yeah, I know you had one even before you started runnin' with Bonnie Jay and I never tole her about Callie. Did you suddenly come to Jesus?"

"Ah, Freddie, no, not really. But I mean, both of them are good girls and that's not really what I need right now."

"I knew it! You talkin' bout busting your cherry, ain't ya? I tole you I know how to fix that."

Freddie Mae was a hardworking woman. She worked for my dad. She worked at Fatman's and for the last three-four years she also "managed" a few ladies of the night who catered to the sexual proclivities of men like my dad. I had a standing offer to do "something" about my condition, but I felt that paying for it was somehow worse than doing it consensually. I did not even go on road trips with my buddies to Juarez where $25 was enough to solve a teenage boy's virgin problem. I just needed a nice girl to understand my needs and to lead me to the Promised Land. Such is the teenage mind. What does love have to do with it? I never thought to ask Freddie why she did what she did or why the world of Odessa was the way it was. Later, when she died, I became sure that the answers to those questions would both explain her death and allow me to exorcise some of my demons. I could not live a life unexamined, so that is why I came back to Odessa, Texas. But first, I had to solve a murder.

Chapter 4
Come September

September 1993

For me, September is always the beginning of a year. School starts. Football two-a-day practices get underway. TV and movies begin to improve from the summer reruns and nonsense. So, the Jencks Law Firm also launched in September. Over the summer, I completed the purchase of the Lee Street building and hired an office manager, Alyce Mayfield, a fifty-something lady who used to be in my mama's Sunday school class and who liked her freedom not to "dress up" as much as I liked UT football. M.A., as everyone called her because she liked her initials backwards, worked at Odessa law firms from the day she finished her Associate degree at Odessa College. She never stayed at one because dressing up always seemed to be required and so did showing up on time. She could not tolerate either, but she noted that no one ever complained that she knew more law than some lawyers and she always finished her work on time and in perfect order.

Her view was that work did not really matter to the "suits." Her being a show pony was what they really wanted except when they got drunk and wanted more. She always warned them that she would "slap you silly" if you touched her and when she did just that to Warren Barnett just after he drunkenly cupped her left breast at a Christmas party, M.A. would not work for any of the lawyers on Court House

Block. That block and those lawyers were Odessa's elite. Lee Street was five blocks and a world away from the Block. She agreed to work for me because I interviewed her wearing jeans and a Permian jersey-oh, and because she loved my mama.

M.A. was an important hire that summer but Jack Fields, Little Jack, was even more important. Jack and I had been friends since the third grade at Alamo Elementary. Jack was a skinny and awkward kid through the 8th grade at Bonham, but his ninth-grade year, he grew up and filled in. By high school, he was a beast. He played center and he could get off the ball faster than most guards and he never stopped blocking his man or someone else's man until the ref blew his whistle (or sometimes after the whistle). He hustled so much that he once opened a hole for the fullback on a draw play, got knocked down, got up and ran down the field, and hit the defensive back just before he prevented our winning touchdown against the Midland JV. The film drew raves from the coaches and varsity but also earned me unwanted derision. As Jack was heroically saving the day, the film clearly showed me just standing at the scrimmage line, hands on my hips, watching his exploits. All I could say was that I knew Little Jack had it all the way. Play like that all the way through high school earned Jack a football scholarship to the University of Houston, a football school, where Jack never played a down. In his first week of practice at Houston, he bent down to lace his shoes and his right lung collapsed. He stayed in school, did well, and then attended Texas Tech law school where he mastered Oil and Gas Law. Of the latter, I knew absolutely nothing. I hired him over the phone.

24

Jack and M.A. were smarter than any officer I met in the Army or any lawyer I worked with at Stanley. I admit that I never considered that possibility. Both occasionally wore cowboy boots and talked with an intentionally ungrammatical twang. Neither went to a "good" school. Both stayed in Odessa. M.A. was a churchgoer and Jack got married just before graduating high school. He was still married to the same girl/woman, Dana. Now I asked you, does any of this sound smart? Granted Jack used to stump me in high school by using words like "egregious" or "omniscient," but I never saw his name on the Honor Roll. Wait, did I ever look for any other name but my own? Our friendship was not based on smarts and by our junior year I was more concerned with girls than with my buddies. Maybe I missed something. As for M. A., a lady almost twenty years older who usually wore western dresses and went to Sunday School just did not catch my eye or my interest. One thing I did learn in the Army and in D.C. though: Someone has to do the work. The last oil bust in Odessa made two workhorses available to me, so I grabbed them up. Now could we make enough money in Odessa to keep us all in tamales?

Chapter 5
Law and Order

Driving to work on Tuesday, September 7, 1993, I felt both energized and a bit undone. I was a boss. In my head was a long list of how not to be a boss, but what to do as boss was beyond me. Then there was Jack. How do I boss around the guy who drove me home, put me to bed, and then chatted up my mom as I lay down to sleep off my first adventure with a bottle of sweet banana wine we had found at his house? Still the sickest I have ever been, but Mama believed Jack when he told her that I had just been puking up his concoction of Tiger's Milk (a yeast-based energy drink) and Dr. Pepper. He said he made it because it was a health drink prescribed by a Dr. It would be good to see my ole buddy even if I didn't know exactly how this new relationship would work out.

And now as I pulled into the office driveway expecting to see an old friend, there was a man right there on the building's small porch. I took it that his pickup was the one parked on the street. But was it Jack? This guy was bearded, heavy, and, of all things, smoking a cigarette. When I hired Jack in a phone interview, he was away from Odessa at Lake Brownwood indulging his passions for fishing and lying to his buddies. He sounded like Jack. He joked and told stories like Jack. Still, I had not seen him in probably ten-plus years. But this guy? This guy looked like someone who had been rode hard and put up wet.

"Covey Jencks, you rascal," the fellow yelled out. "What do you do on a 47 inside reverse?"

"Pull left and kick out on the defensive right end if Courtney remembers to block down on the tackle," I said as I man-hugged this stranger who still recalled our JV offense.

"Right you are, and I block your man!" shouted Jack.

"Who the hell are you, Mountain Man? I was expecting 'Lil Jack'."

"He's long gone, Cove. Now I am just one biscuit shy of 235 pounds, and I am havin' that for lunch today now we are working together again!"

A word about Jack. He's a charmer and he's also never going to reveal anything really important, including his intelligence. My phone interview with him was typical. We talked for forty-five minutes and I only really got two solid pieces of information. He was available for hire and he had not yet been disbarred. I had to learn from a mutual friend that in oil bust of the mid-80s he had managed to hold onto a job only due to Old Man Tubby Ted Daniell's loyalty to his old players. Ted had once been our JV coach but had long left coaching for insurance, not oil and gas, and Jack became his glorified gofer, not a lawyer.

During the mid-80s downturn, no occupation was safe from the ravages of the collapse. The price of West Texas crude in 1986 had dropped by 58 % to about $10 a barrel virtually overnight and that collapse reverberated through all of Texas but especially in West Texas. Jack was a typical victim. Why he even stayed in Odessa is anyone's guess, but I suspect Dana loved Odessa and Jack loved Dana, so he stayed. Then there's the fact that many West Texans think of Odessa as a great place to live and, hell, in the oil "bidness" whatever goes down always comes back up. The truth is that I offered Jack his first lawyer's job in 7 years. That is a good thing because Tubby Ted died on an operating table just last spring. Jack had not worked in months and the price of oil still struggled under $20.00 a barrel.

If I had doubted how to manage my relationship with Jack, he did me one better as soon as we pushed passed the leftover furniture and two empty desks that the last occupants (business unknown) had walked away from. Before I could suggest going out for coffee or even starting to put the place in order, Jack put it to me squarely.

"What the hell, Covey?"

"Sorry," I said.

"This place is a mess, Cove. You expecting me to clean all this up and even hang out our shingles? I thought you said we were setting up a law firm?"

"Yes, Jack, sure, I mean, I just figured we'd work together to make this happen. I just walked in this place for the first time, too."

"Let me get this straight. You quit that fancy firm in D.C. last spring. Came back to Odessa early summer. Bought this building, you said in early July, but never walked in here 'til after Labor Day?"

"When you put it like that, Jack, it doesn't sound reasonable."

"You know, me and Dana been trying to figure you out the last few weeks, Covey. You give up a dream job in D.C. to come back to Odessa after acting like you were better than West Texas for, I don't know, even before you left here in the first place."

"What, no, what do you mean?"

"Covey, your senior year you quit football. You dropped out of our Hi Y Club. You barely spoke you your old friends and you never even said goodbye when you left for College. I only knew you were in law school when one day my daddy saw your daddy at Furr's cafeteria."

"Jack, no, I mean my last year of high school was very hard on me and I just got caught up in my school and work. I was disconnected. Then there was the war and…"

"Bull Shit, Covey. When you left Odessa, you left Odessa. Coming back don't make sense. And to go into oil and gas? U.T. Law is great and all, but it is theoretical and intellectual stuff from what I hear. You ever take a class in Oil and Gas law?"

"No."

"What was you workin' on at Stanley?"

"Insurance."

"In the Army, you worked in..?"

"Acquisitions."

"In the immortal words of every dumbass in West Texas, 'What the fuck, Jencks?' I mean I will take your $25,000 a year, but I can't see how long this can last or what the hell we are doing. Can you tell me what's going on?"

So, unlike me, Jack had grown up. I had expected to explain myself over time, but I figured it would not be the first day in the first hour. Jack reasonably enough wanted to know what he was getting into and I was about to tell him when the door flew open and in walked a Texas tornado in human form, M.A. I barely had time to notice her turquoise squaw's dress and brown cowboy boots with turquoise flowers. Her dirty blonde hair was barely combed, but overall, she looked like a damned handsome woman. But I barely had time to notice.

"Well, if it isn't Twiddle Dee and Twiddle Dumber. What are y'all doin' standing around in this dump?"

"M.A., good morning. We were about to set this place right. I just wanted to get your input about how to lay out the office. Say, do you know Jack Fields?"

"They nodded, and both laughed."

"Jencks, I have known this fella since he was ten years old. I used to be the scorekeeper for the Odessa Little League and Jack had the highest batting average any ten-year-old ever had. What was it, Little Jack, .600?"

"It was .500, 5 for 10, and I almost never played. Baseball was not really my thing. Glad to see you, Ms. Mayfield. You might also tell Covey that we worked together a few months over at Blankenship and Blankenship 'til the bottom fell out. I said yes to Covey here because I knew you'd be here."

"Yeah, me and the fact that you ain't been employed for a while now."

"Yeah, that too," Jack smiled.

There you have it. I was the outsider in my own business. From Day One this gang would be all about truth-telling. That, of course, is not my strong suit. Stanley, the Army, UT, none of those places really required it. Just work the situation, be yourself in your own head, and don't bother us. These West Texans were having none of it.

"Covey was about to tell me why he came back to Odessa, M.A. I mean it makes ya wonder if he couldn't make the cut or do the work in D.C. And how does he have the money to hire us? And why does he want to do oil and

30

gas when among our group of friends, he was the only one who had no one in the family in the "bidness." He don't know a pump jack from an oil derrick. Hell, back in school, he didn't even own a pair of boots to wear to Western Week. I figure he's a Democrat as well."

"Yeah, Covey, your mama told me that you loved it at college and at law school. Why didn't you take your weird-self back to Austin instead of here? And is Jack right? Do you have the money to get us going? If not, I am going to go back to teaching computer science at OHS. At least I get some benefits."

"Damn, you folks are a tough crowd with all the questions, but, grab a chair. This may take 'til lunch, but I will tell you what you need, I mean, deserve to know."

It did not take until lunch, but I told them. Yes, I had the money to open the office and it was not all from my law firm salary. My dad, who was in a nursing home over in Monahans, had written me a check for $107,000 back in May. It was to bring his assets below the amount that allowed him to qualify for Medicaid and go to the nursing home. That was not illegal then, but it was clearly unethical. In June, the doctors had told me that he was never leaving that nursing home, so in fact, the money was mine to keep. Also, when Mama, divorced and alone, died in '87, she had $30,000 in the bank which she had taken from the car wash profits over 12 years when she did the books and the banking for her "nere do well" husband. I had $55,000 from the Army, the clerkship, and Stanley.

"You think nearly $200,000 can buy us a year or two to get going?

"How much for this fine establishment?" asked M.A.

"$12,500 cash out outright, but I paid out of my Stanley bonus money."

"No computer. No access to Lexus Nexus. No supplies really of any kind. What's my budget to get us in working order?" asked M.A.

"What do you need?"

"Jack, you still keep the Texas law journals you had at Blankenship?" she asked.

"Sure," he said.

"Covey, I figure you don't know a Macintosh from an IBM Clone, right?"

"Right," I said.

"So, I'm telling you now that a computer is not a fancy typewriter. It is a 'word processor' and the internet is bigger, easier to use, and more practical than that set of the British Encyclopedia your mama bought you in high school. We have to have a good one. Understand?"

"M.A., I know. The paralegals in D.C. told me all about it."

"OK, with the understanding that we have to have a computer with all the necessary applications, decent furniture, and passable heating and air in this place, and don't forget insurance, right o' way, I need $5,000-$6,000, maybe a little less or a little more. With unemployment taxes, utilities, advertising, and use of our own vehicles, we can last no more than 18 months if we don't have any business, but we need business. I'm assuming you do *not* have a business plan, right Jencks?"

"Right."

"Then I agree with Jack. What in the hell are you doing here?"

I wanted to say that I was in a quest for truth, but that phrase rang hollow in my head when I realized how selfish I had been. This enterprise was not just for me. Two others and the others who depended on them were involved. What had I done? I started with, "Thanks for your honesty and let me tell you why I am here."

Oh, I did reassure them that I am a real lawyer and a generally smart person. I learned things in the Army and I got an education doing insurance cases, but I was back in Odessa to solve a murder that explains why I had been a lost soul for so long. I was not sure, really, how I felt about Odessa, but I hated D.C. and I was wary of a life in politics and the politics of life in Austin. This whole thing was an experiment. I ended with:

"I don't know how long we can last, but my family's life's savings will help us get off the ground. I will work hard to learn from both of you. I will take a minimal salary. You are in fact the company."

M.A. smiled. Jack relaxed and then said:

"Covey, my man, I sorta like it. M.A. and I talked about working together way back in the day when we were stuck with rich assholes. I also knew in high school that Freddie Mae's death upset your whole applecart. You've got issues and I am not surprised to hear you can't let it go. And you know the best part?"

"You have new information about her murder?"

"Hell no! I think her husband did it like everyone else did at the time. The best part is that Odessa is going to come back again soon because of Middle East politics and advances in oil field technology. The technology will open up access to old and new deposits and political instability will jack up oil prices. Ten years from now, or less, Odessa will boom, again. If we stay small and get ready, we can make it. Your timing is almost perfect. If you stick with it and stay out of the way, we might just survive."

Not the last time Jack turned out to be an optimistic savant. Who knew?

Chapter 6
The Plan

When M.A. talked about a business plan and Jack opined on oil field technology, I was not as disconnected from reality as my answers suggested. I did not have a formal business plan, but I had a plan on how to do business in West Texas. And while I was totally unaware of advances in directional drilling and fracking in the oil field, I was aware of how automated technology could transform a business and affect its employers and employees. My formal education may have occurred at Austin College and matured at U.T. Law, but my practical education came at my daddy's knees in Odessa, Texas. From 1964-1982, my dad owned 1, 2, and then 3 car washes in West Texas. Over that time, my dad's enterprises went from 30-40 employees a weekend down to 6-10. They went from washing 300 cars a week to washing well over 750 per location per week. His businesses went from offering car washes to selling gas and washes, to vehicle detailing, to steam cleaning and painting motors, to polishing, painting and keeping up truck and car fleets from miles around. My daddy was Car Wash King of West, by God, Texas.

From the beginning he innovated. He added gasoline tanks and pumps to offer gas to customers as well as a wash, and he went from there to lowering the price of gas to lure in customers. Folks said that he started every gas war in Odessa for a decade and once he took it down to as low as 8 cents a gallon. That earned him a lot of customers but not many friends in the many service stations around

35

town. Later he reversed the process and lowered the price of the wash based on the volume of gas a person bought. Eighteen gallons gave you a car wash for 59 cents. More customers, fewer friends. By the late sixties, he worked out arrangements with car dealers through which they brought their new vehicles to our place for detailing instead of doing it in-house. We closed the car wash on Wednesdays to drop in customers.

We got bigger and bigger, but the technology handwriting was on the wall by the late 60s. Daddy could see that in other places in the U.S. car washes were investing in equipment that automated steam cleaning the tires, soaping and buffing the car's body, and drying off the water. On top of that this equipment came to work every day; did a consistent job; and never asked if he could hire someone's cousin. He needed money to buy this stuff though, so he got a plan.

He would sell one of his two car washes in 1968, at a discount, of course, but for cash. He got $30,000 for his first place on Old Dixie, Frank's Car Wash, and invested most of that money on automating the place on North Andrews Highway. At first, it did not work because folks in town still went to Frank's out of habit but then the guy who had bought it dropped dead of a heart attack. His family sold it back to my dad for $10,000 since they knew nothing about managing a rack. Daddy scavenged some to the equipment but then closed the place. He sold a lot of stuff to Mexican car washes just to get more cash. The new equipment started going in on Andrews Highway in '73, so the timing was good. How could 1973 be a good time? War and oil-shock you say? Quadrupling of oil prices and depression you say? Not in West Texas. Oil prices go up, West Texas booms.

That period began a decade of boom and growth in West Texas and a period of financial fortune for my family. One rack became two as we put one in Midland and then three as we put one in Abilene. Each was a success. I did not understand all this because I was a kid, but later it made sense. Have a good product, discount prices, keep looking for ways to lower overhead, always innovate technologically, think of new ways to provide services, and most of all, be lucky as hell. Money and friends were fungible, so only spend when you need to, but, when you need to, spend. Oh, and hire people who know your business and the balls to keep it growing.

That was my daddy's business plan and it was what I had in mind in 1993. You think my daddy ever washed a car himself over the 18 years he owned car washes? Not very many, my friend, not very many. He was a true Cowboy Capitalist.

Chapter 7
Six Months Later

The office was humming. Jack was reviewing Slade's "Primer on Oil and Gas Law of Texas, 2nd edition." Our new, meagerly-paid, intern from the University, UT-Permian Basin, Erica Garza, was printing oil company organization charts for our perusal. M.A. was sitting at her desk taking notes from Satira Alberts, office manager of Watts and Company Drilling, as she dished on the issues that her company had with their lawyers and the (relatively) high fees they charged for (relatively) easy transactions. Watts had become our first place to try to convince to let us save them money. Not only was Satira M.A.'s good friend, but John Edward Watts had played ball with Jack. With me too, but frankly I did not count. Jack figured we could draw up sales contracts for a fraction of what Watts was currently paying, and tightwad that he was he'd take our offer. But we all wanted it to be Edward's idea, not ours. We also cared more about securing the business than the amount we made. We had an in; we had a plan; and we were patiently preparing our campaign. How I wished I could focus as much on solving Freddie's murder as I did the price of West Texas crude.

"Hello, Counselor."

Jack always called me counselor when I had provided not a lick of legal work in days.

"Where ya been?"

Dang, he didn't even look up.

"You'd be proud. I went over to the Petroleum Museum in Midland. I know all about the geological history of the Permian Sea and the carbon deposits close to the Matador Arch," I proudly declared.

"Yeah, you did," Jack replied. "Was that before or after you trapped Bo Gladstone at the 'Coffee Shop' over on Grant Ave.? I watched you for thirty minutes and you never even had a clue I was there."

"Hmmm, well..."

"Go ahead; you were pumping him for information about Freddie Mae's death since Bo's older brother found her, right?"

"Right."

"Them two boys were a piece of work, weren't they? I remember Bo askin' if Odessa had a KKK."

He paused. "I teased him that he wanted to set up a branch at Permian High School, like maybe the Junior Klansmen. For a half second, he took me serious. "

"Well, he hasn't changed, but I needed to know things that I was too out of it to ask in '79?"

"Like what?" asked Jack.

"Like, was there a real investigation into Freddie's murder? Was there real evidence against Freddie's husband, Cleon? Did they ever figure why she was found on the grounds of an old barn next to a working oil patch? And what about that knife?"

"Bo smart enough or care enough to answer?"

"Yeah, right, both valid questions," I said. "This was, in fact, my second meeting with him. At the first, I had to convince him to go ask Brother Dan. I have no access to any written documents and I refuse to get anywhere close to Dan."

"Why would he help you, Cove? He's gotta know you are ACLU material all the way and he used to bully you up and down every street of Odessa, Texas. He's no friend."

"No, but he's in insurance now and he has some social standing. I just happen to be the guy he came to when he stole an upcoming Biology test junior year and threatened to stomp on me if I didn't give him the answers. Remember Tubby Ted had a no pass, no play rule."

"You blackmailed him!" he exclaimed

"Oh, hell no, but the fact is when we first re-connected he actually apologized for bullying me all those years. I graciously accepted his apology, but I mentioned the Biology incident and I told him he since he owed me one, I'd trade acceptance of his apology for information."

Jack responded, "And that worked?"

"Oh, hell yes. That and I told him that he might get our insurance business at Jencks and Associates but I'd for sure buy a term life insurance policy from him if he got me answers."

Jack smiled "And?"

"Capitalist whore that he is he got me answers."

Chapter 8
How It Went Down in '79

Freddie Mae's murder may not have made the newspaper, but the Odessa Police did not ignore it. The reason was football. In 1979 Odessa Permian had only had a marginally integrated football team for 4 years but the black players had an immediate impact. Daryl Hunt, the first such player, had been a great player at Permian and went on to OU to become an All American. As everyone could see, there was a pipeline of "colored" backs, wideouts, and linebackers that could upgrade the football team and guarantee more championships. Best yet; they lived in Odessa and boosters didn't have to provide their daddies' jobs to lure them to town.

The Police wanted to clear up Freddie's case from the start to show that her death was no "racial incident." That she was found in the marginally white side of town caused concern. The cops knew some white men (and some of whom were prominent) visited Fatman's BBQ on occasion and they knew Freddie had a "side job" of running working girls. The white women of Odessa need not be bothered with such details if none of their husbands were involved in Freddie's death. And black folks need not fear to send their boys to the east side to play football. The hope was that Freddie's death was not the start of "somethin'." That hope, and the police's intent were to keep Freddie's death a south side issue only and one that would not disturb decent folks. But they'd take the investigation where it led.

The "lucky" part of their investigation was a witness, Mr. James "No Nose" Jackson. Since a childhood illness, Jackson had no sense of smell, but he had a good sense of hearing and he had a nearly constant thirst. As a result, he hung out at Fatman's BBQ just about every night. He liked the live music and he loved the cold beer. The Police traced Freddie's movements the night she died and indeed she had been at Fat's as late as 10:00 PM and No Nose had been there before 10 and well after 10.

Detective Junior Baker, a 15-year veteran of the force and a former Marine, interviewed No Nose, but such as things were in Odessa at the time, both the detective and the black man felt like the interview was an adversarial encounter. Baker held the upper hand and No Nose could not ask for a lawyer even if at times he felt he needed one.

Baker: "You say you saw Freddie Mae Johnson on Friday, March 21, 1979?"

No Nose: "I...I did. Yes, sir, I did."

Baker: "Where and when?"

No Nose: "Over to Fatman's along about 10."

Baker: "Who else was there at the time?"

No Nose: "Well, let me see. Hard to recollect all tha names. There was John Wesley, you know the Fatman hisself, and Laverne, his ole lady, and..."

Baker, impatiently interrupting: "Mr. Jackson, were there any white men there?"

No Nose: "White folks on Friday night? No, never. They night is Sunday night. You know when most decent peoples are in church."

Baker, ignoring the dig: "Just tell me, was Freddie there with anyone?"

42

No Nose: "Uh, no not really 'les you count her no good husband, Cleon. He was there alone fussing at Miss Freddie."

Baker: "Fussing?"

No Nose: "Well, I heard him yell at her onct."

Baker: "Tell me what he was yellin' about?"

No Nose: "Oh, what he always be sayin' to Freddie, 'Bitch, I'm gonna cut you!'"

That testimony, verified by three others, sealed Cleon's fate. The police investigation proved that Freddie and Cleon often argued and often resorted to more than words, though they did not reveal that the one time either of them went to Odessa Medical Center's ER, it was Cleon and not Freddie. They also did not reveal that "I'm going cut you" was Cleon's favorite phrase to anyone with whom he was angry and, yet, he never cut anyone in his life-perhaps until Freddie. Nevertheless, like many black men in Odessa, he did have a "record."

As a young man, he had broken into a boat shop and stolen a motor he tried to sell for spending money.

Hearing Bo's recounting of the evidence after the fact and through brother's Dan's exaggerations it still seemed that the Police reasoning was solid. Cleon threatened her. Police knew that most murders are crimes of passion and the spouse is always the first suspect. That the threat occurred hours before the body was found, that Freddie was in night clothes, that her body was nowhere close to Fatman's or to her home were never explained. The Bowie knife was never linked to Cleon. There were no fingerprints. Cleon's court-appointed attorney was more interested in getting the rap reduced to a manslaughter sentence and clearing his docket than finding what really happen. Cleon was also resigned to a guilty verdict knowing Odessa and being an ex-con. He was glad not to get the death sentence and he knew he'd be back to Odessa in the not too distant future. It was the times he lived in, but hearing it all in 1993, I was even more determined to find out what really happened. Somehow, I thought Freddie's death did not actually unfold on a Friday night but perhaps many months before.

Chapter 9
Odessa, 1978

I remember that Saturday morning, in mid-June, 1978, like it was yesterday. It was already 80 degrees at 7:30 AM and there was a shimmer in the air that I always assumed was oil or natural gas film reflecting in the morning sunlight. Little flashes of blue or red appeared and disappeared around me as I drove down 27th Street on my way to work on Andrews highway. My hatred of working on Summer Saturdays was somewhat mitigated by the fact that the night before had been a good one. I played in an American Legion baseball game and hit a home run. Afterward, Nancy Schackleford, the cutest blonde cheerleader at Permian, had congratulated me and smiled what I thought was a "call me sometime and maybe we could go to the bushes together" smile. Nancy never cared who a boy was "going with." If she wanted him, she got him. I was wondering to myself if I could be had when I pulled into the car wash lot.

The rack opened in less than thirty minutes and not one employee could be seen installing the vacuum hoses, hauling out the wash rags, removing the locks from gas pumps, or testing the various workstations' equipment to certify that all was in working order. I knew that everyone was there because all the help's cars were parked way in the back of the lot up against the short pipe wall that separated the car wash from the neighborhood houses behind us. My first thought was "Damn, I am going to have to scramble to get the place ready," but my second thought was "What the hell is going on?"

I didn't pull back to the wall. Instead, I went to the end of the rack close to the storage room. In times of trouble, folks went there to talk privately and vent their emotions. True to form, angry voices emanated from behind a closed door where it was probably over 90 degrees and the people speaking seemed considerably hotter.

"Mr. Frank can't do this!"

"He killin' this rack and the peoples in it!"

"God Damn, I 'ma goin' quit, too!"

Opening the door, the Guys were there-John Wesley, James, Gro, Rosa and Freddie Mae. The men were talking, Rosa was sitting next to a crying Freddie Mae, and I was entirely welcome even though I was the boss' son. I was one of the Guys.

I spoke to the real leader of Frank's Number 2 Car Wash, Gro.

"What's my daddy done now, Gro?"

"Covey, Junior, you gotta talk to your daddy. He laid off Freddie Mae for no account."

"You're kidding me? Shit!"

Everyone knew Frank could pretty well do as he pleased. He was King; the Guys actually called him "the Kingfish." He had pared back employees ruthlessly and easily for several years now, but the core group seemed untouchable. They ran the place. In fact, they often told others who was being hired or who was being fired. They kept discipline on the rack; they came early and stayed late; and they kept secrets that needed keeping. One secret was my dad's on again, off again, sexual dalliances with Freddie

46

Mae. We all thought she was untouchable in part because of her relationship with Frank, but also because she was mother confessor and fixer to everyone there, including me. She knew everything about me. What girls I liked. How I hated the car wash business. What grades I made. What bullies I was afraid of. And every aspect of my sexual development. My dad knew that Gro was the boss, but Freddie Mae was the heart and soul of Frank's Car Wash number 2. She was more than that to me. She was the one person in life I could talk to about my hopes, fears, and big plans. She had over the previous five years replaced either of my parents as the person to whom I sought approval and from whom I received unconditional love. Little did I know that she was equally important to many other persons, but all that mattered to me was that she was my rock and the person on whom I depended most.

"I will talk to him," I said. "Today! As soon as he comes in. No matter how busy we are. That Motherfucker!"

Freddie stiffened up, "Think straight, Boy. That just sets you offen him. We don't need no squabble in the front office during business."

She thought a second, and wiped her nose with a Kleenex and said:

"Gro, this is your job. I don't know why he done it, but once Frank decides, there ain't no turnin' back. I don't want anyone else losin' a job 'cause of me. You all got families who depend on you. I can take care of myself, but I want some consideration, you know, for the years I put in and for things, you know."

We knew.

Chapter 10 Come to Jesus

The Friendship Baptist Church is two blocks over the tracks on the west side of South Dixie. Its faded brown brick façade masks a large chapel with faded wooden benches, an impressive choir loft, and tall pulpit that accommodates a tall preacher. The door to the right of the pulpit at floor level leads to Reverend Leroy Williams' inner and outer offices where I would now step back in time to try to reconstruct the night Freddie died. Lucky for me Cleon Johnson had been working there as the maintenance man ever since his release from Huntsville prison in 1989. He could have gotten out earlier, but he was once denied parole for being a two-time offender and once he could not show up for a parole hearing because he was laid up in a hospital bed after an "incident" with another inmate who happened to be in a "Mexican gang." He had not hardened from being in prison; he had retreated. Reverend Leroy took him in; gave him a bed; and paid him food money. Cleon had given up drink, had never taken drugs, and believed completely in the healing power of Jesus. But he virtually never left the grounds of his church and every single Church Lady there held Cleon in the highest regard. You can be sure that Cleon never wanted for fried chicken and greens on Sunday and he never sought any undue comfort from any person, male or female.

To find what the Odessa Police missed in 1979, I went to see Cleon first since he surely held the key to Freddie's death. I knew the answer to my intended first question, but as we sat in Reverend Leroy's outer office next to copies of the *Baptist Standard*, children's coloring books with Biblical themes, and very old *Jet Magazines*, Cleon was also ready.

We exchanged handshakes, his a medium soft, almost apologetic grasp, and mine white-man firm. Cleon's hair was now completely gray, but his thin build and narrow shoulders were just the same as they were in 1978, the last time I saw him.

"Thanks for meeting me, Mr. Johnson. You know Freddie meant so much to me."

"Please, folks just call me Cleon, Mr. Covey."

"...and I am just Covey."

"You meant the world to Alfreda. You was like a son to her."

"I know. And she meant everything to me. I also know you didn't kill her, but I wonder if you have any idea who did."

"No, I did not kill her, but I take responsibility for her death."

"How so?"

"I left her at Fatman's that bad night and I knew she was all agitated about somethin'. She was tryin' to tell me about it, but all's I wanted was more drink, always more drink. My Mama called it demon rum and that demon got holt of me. I said bad things to my woman 'cause she ain't give me no money. I cursed her. I threatened her. Some fool did give me the money and I commenced to get drunker. Hours later, still drunk, I set out to find her, but I passed out in my car as I was fixin' to go look for her. In that condition I couldn't help Alfreda and I couldn't help my own self. Hell, the Po-lice found me sleepin' right there the next mornin'. They say I killed her and came right back to Fat's but how I gonna drive in that condition?"

"You have any idea why she was agitated?"

49

"No idea. No idea at all. I mean, it's no secret that she and I were, how you say, separated, so I didn't know that much. I didn't even know Kingfish, I mean your daddy, let her go. I just knowed she had money and I needed me some to feed my bad habits. I sure am sorry I cain't help you much, Mr. Covey."

I stood and patted Cleon on the shoulder.

"Cleon, you have helped a lot. Just so you know, I am proud what you have done with your life."

I reached for my wallet and Cleon held up his hand.

"No, sir, Mr. Covey, no sir. My own two feet. Always my own two feet, but if you want to come back here for services like you done back then, you are mighty welcome."

I smiled that he recalled.

"How's the choir, Cleon?"

"Better than ever. You come see."

"I will, Cleon, I promise. God bless you."

Walking away from Friendship Church, Odessa, Texas came rushing back to me. This church I occasionally attended with B.J. Those ladies in big, colorful, beautiful hats on Sunday mornings. Reverend Leroy's two-hour sermons while I waxed anxious about missing parts of Dallas Cowboys' games. That world that co-existed with my white world and, yet, it was the one I missed when I thought of Odessa.

And one other thought. If Freddie Mae had money just months after Frank fired her, where did she get it?

Chapter 10
As Luck Would Have It

M.A. never ceased to amaze me. There I was pondering the mysteries of 1978 and the whos and whys of Odessa and there she was in a pink western shirt, dark blue jeans, and black flats. Her hair was pulled back. I barely had time to notice.

"Covey, you got a call," she said excitedly.

"Did you send in the insurance payment this month?"

"It may be a good call, Goofball. You recall the name Ranger Hauling Company over to Abilene?"

"Ranger, limme see, Ranger? Yeah, I think my daddy did their trucks at the Abilene wash back when."

"Yep, and?"

"And what, Ms. Mayfield, and what?"

It turns out that time and space are relative things. The West Texas of the 60s and 70s, Austin College of the 80s, and Odessa of the 90s were not separate and distinct realities. As I was learning every day, they were connected and today I learned that I personally had connections.

This time to someone's relative who at college was my friend and my friend's father had done business with my daddy. At Luckett Hall in Sherman, the guy with the best pick-up basketball game in Sid Richardson Gym and the best pick-up lines with girls was Tommy "Two Tone" Franklin. Two years my senior and a Philosophy/Religion major, Tommy had a way with girls and a dope connection in Dallas that kept Luckett third floor stoked every

51

weekend. What I now learned was that Tommy came from Abilene, that his daddy was Thomas Franklin of Ranger Hauling Company, that Mr. Franklin knew I was the Car Wash King's boy even back then, and that Tommy, rascal of all rascals, was now Assistant Chaplain of Mo-Ranch Presbyterian Assembly down in beautiful south central Texas. Mr. Franklin knew two more things--that I "came" from D.C. but was now back in Odessa.

Pleasantries aside, the gist of my call to Thomas Franklin changed the course of Jencks and Associates Law Firm, saved it really, and substantially delayed my investigation into Freddie's death.

"Mr. Franklin," I said at what I thought was the end of our call, "give Tommy my best and tell him that I may someday drop in on him down in Kerrville."

"You bet, Covey. Now let's talk business."

Oh yeah, business. Thomas Franklin was a sophisticated businessman. His company was a real player in the Texas trucking industry and that industry had suffered with others during the downturn. But there was a new game in town. It was called the North American Free Trade Agreement (NAFTA). In a nutshell, NAFTA meant more imports and exports would flow through Texas and roughly 90 percent of the goods going both ways would travel by trucks. Franklin and Ranger Hauling wanted two things to happen: 1) Texas companies would haul those goods and 2) West Texas haulers would get their "fair share" of business, so the Big City haulers could not be allowed to corner the market. And Franklin wanted to know two other things from me: 1) Could I get up to speed on NAFTA? and 2) While I was in D.C., did I learn how

52

"Washington works"? The West Texas lawyer's answer to both questions was "Oh, hell yes!" In fact, what I was to learn was that NAFTA was the 1993-1998 "West Texas Lawyers' Relief Fund." We were in the tamales if we could get it right. Franklin had uttered the magic word, "retainer."

We went into to full court press. Jack would steep himself in NAFTA's terms and learn all he could about the trucking world and its legal associations. M.A. would get the names and numbers of Kay Bailey Hutchinson's and Phil Gramm's chiefs of staff. She reminded me to add the same for Congressman Chet Edwards' West Texas office. Erica spoke and read Spanish (which the gringo West Texans in the office could navigate only as far as "hola" and "gracias"), so she was off to the Ector County Library to read Mexican newspapers and anything else pertinent to NAFTA's impact on Mexico.

For about six months I was all about meetings with trucking associations, consultations with Congressional staffers, studying National Transportation Safety Board (NTSB) rulings, and nighttime phone calls with my new boss, Thomas Franklin. I have to admit it was the most exciting time I had ever had as a lawyer and I never fell into my bad habits while traveling to D.C. The married women, Camelot Strip Club, and Dupont Villa Bar of D.C. never crossed my mind. More importantly, the gang at Jencks and Associates were working so hard they almost forgot to ask for raises.

Chapter 11
Come Again

Success to the left of me and money to the right, and there I was stuck in the middle with no progress on Freddie's case. Then one Saturday morning NAFTA and Freddie came at me from a totally unexpected direction, Carl Sewell's Toyota Service Center. I was, oh about 5,000 miles past my 20,000-mile maintenance check, so I scheduled one at 8:30 AM. I drove into the facility, told the pretty woman at the customer service desk who I was and what I wanted, walked in the waiting area where the TV had KOSA News on Hyper Blast and starting reading an article in the *Odessa American* on NAFTA's launch since it was mid-1994 and the treaty in its first year was already making an impact on Texas. As I turned the pages, the front page was clearly visible to others in the room. BAM! A man had walked up, seen the article, swatted the back of his hand against my paper, and expressed his opinion in a blunt way.

"You got a Jap car and you're reading about that white nigger's trade deal with them Mexicans! Who do you think you are?"

Now I am an educated and cultured man, so violence never entered my mind. Whippin' his old ass sure did, but I simply stood up and said:

"Back off, Crazy Person, what's wrong with you?"

"You like that NAFTA, fella?"

"Yes, I do, as a matter of fact. How's that your business?"

"I hope a Spic takes your job!"

54

From zero to "let's take it outside" in about 20 seconds. I was just about to tell him that since his mama didn't teach him manners, I was going to beat some into him. Or words to that effect, but I never got there. The customer service lady was suddenly standing there extending her hand to my chest.

"Covey, Covey, hold on now. Wait a second." Then she turned to the maniac and said: "Mr. Peterson, here you go again. What did we say about this? You cannot hit or touch our customers. Now I am going to have to call the facility again, and you have to go back. How did you get over here this mornin? Please sit down relax and take a deep breath. You can't go hittin' on a Permian letterman from back in the day."

The older man turned completely soft. "I'm sorry, Bonnie, I am sorry, I didn't know he was from here and he is drivin' a Jap car and all. I'm sorry, Mister, sometimes I just get all riled up. My daddy died in Iwo Jima. I am sorry."

Bonnie? Bonnie Jay? B.J.? There she was sixteen years older, still beautiful, and totally in charge. Why had I not thought to look for her? Did I assume that she had left Odessa or that she would not talk to me or that...she did not exist except in my memories?

"B.J., I did not recognize you when I came in. Oh, man, I can't believe it. I am so out of it. I am sorry."

"Forget it, Covey, I had no idea who you were either, though of course your picture has been in the papers and everyone on the south side says you are gonna solve Freddie's case. Of course, I had no idea that the first white boy I ever dated, and the first boy I ever really liked, had gone off to conquer the world only to come back, tail between his legs, to find the son-of-a-bitch who killed the kindest, most wonderful, person in the world. I had no idea you had a law office over to Lee Street and that your daddy is in the nursing home in Monahans. No idea."

"So you pretty much hate me twice over. Once for 1978 and once again for 1993."

"I don't hate you. I don't even know you. And you sure as hell don't know me, but I can't have you fighting old guys from the rest home over yonder while decent folks all around you are just sitting here quietly have their morning coffee."

"Would you sit down and have coffee with me?"

"Absolutely not!"

I started to apologize again, but words failed me. I could not believe any of what had just happened. I wanted to leave but had no car. I wanted to start over, but I had already blown it. I wanted to hide, but there was only empty space. There I was exposed and flabbergasted. But B.J. was still there too.

"Well then, what about dinner?" I blurted. The teenage girl in tight skirts had grown into a beauty in black slacks and light blue Carl Sewell company shirt, with the edges of a darker blue lacy bra peeking out. Something stirred inside me.

"What about my husband and two babies?" she retorted.

"Uh, them too."

"I'm actually not married."

"Is it tough with two kids?"

"Yes, but they are my sister's?"

"Ben's Little Mexico?"

56

"Hell no! It's Frank Green's Barn Door Steakhouse over on North Grant Street or Luigi's in Midland or nothing at all. Ben's later."

"Are we dating again?"

"No sir! I might give you a trial run to see if you have a shred of human decency left in your lawyer's body, but the thing is, we need to talk."

"Really, you mean you will give me another chance after…"

"Hush, what happens when you are 17 just don't count. Besides Freddie told me why you ran away from me and she told me your sordid secrets. Had things not gotten so crazy, I was going to talk to you about my side of the story."

"Really? Tell me."

"Wine, Covey, candles on tables, soft light, and slow music, and a long conversation. One I have been hopin' for a few months now. You man enough to handle it?"

"Oh, hell yes."

Chapter 12
Guilty as Charged

Callie Mae used to say that I thought too much. I can't deny it. I think, and I worry too much. Right after seeing B.J. my mind was in turmoil. Why had I ditched her back then? Why had I not looked for her? Why had I not recognized her? I felt guilt and shame over these things, but there was more. Does she want a relationship? I don't have time for a relationship, but I am horny, my God, am I horny. What is it, 18 months since…, but no way am I going to take advantage of her and then make up some reason to dump her again. But what about my pledge of independence? What about what an incredible woman she seems? Perhaps she has information about Freddie. She was Freddie's friend. Maybe she could help. But…but…but. Guilt, shame. And contrary thoughts.

Such thoughts did not dissuade me from trying to look good. Not D.C. good with a black pinstripe suit and a shirt with French cuffs but Texas formal: blue jeans, white button-down shirt, and a blue blazer. The cowboy boots might have been a bit much, but there they were.

As much as I wanted to take B.J. to Odessa's best first-date restaurant, Tom Green's Barn Door Steakhouse on the edge of downtown, I chose Luigi's in Midland instead. It is smaller, quieter, and more romantic. Better yet, it is twenty miles away, so there'd be more time for talking coming and going. Her blue strapless dress would make it hard to concentrate on the road though. Why, oh why, did she choose a red lacy bra? Does she not have any regard for public safety on the Texas highways? Going over, B.J. quizzed me on especially the Army and D.C. I tried to focus on her, but she deflected our conversation away from my comments and my compliments. When we got to Luigi's, she really set me straight. Seconds after being seated:

"We are not dating Covey Jencks. We are getting reacquainted."

"OK, sure, B.J."

"And stop calling me B.J. I don't like the connotation and I also don't like Bonnie Jay or Bonnie. Call me what my mama called me, JayJay, or just J."

"OK, what do your friends call you?"

"What I ask them to call me, OK?"

"Yep."

The waiter approached and JayJay commanded, "Yes, waiter, red wine for both of us. I'll have veal scaloppini. Covey, what you havin'?"

"Lasagna, thanks."

"And no garlic bread, OK, sir?"

(Is there hope?)

She continued as he stepped away.

"Here's the truth. I have always known more about you than you have known about me. I was shy back then and didn't know how to tell a boy what I liked or wanted. I am grown up now."

"That's a fact."

"Just listen. There are some things I been wantin' to tell you all these years. The main thing you don't know is that as bad as your daddy truly was, mine was worse. What he did to my older sister and what he almost did to me was beyond awful. Sister may never recover. My mama knew

59

all about it and did nothing. From the time I was 11 Freddie protected me. That was the age he started messin' with Sister, and Freddie made my mama let me sleep at her house across the street. I had my own key."

I was gob-smacked. JayJay was, in fact, my key to unlocking Freddie's mystery. She went on.

Freddie not only protected her, she made J promise to tell if her daddy ever touched her, and Freddie told J's old man to his face in front of his wife that if he ever tried to "spoil" JayJay, she'd get someone to cut off his thing. J wanted out of the house almost as soon as she graduated high school; she married Charles Qualls, Ector High's smartest boy at 19, both to get out of the house and to take his last name, but they divorced 4 years later when the union produced no kids and no sparks. JayJay went to Odessa College, studied business methods, and got a job at Odessa's most prestigious car dealership from 1987 on. She was the first African-American on the "floor" at Sewell's and she was a hit with everyone from the start.

I asked how everything was now. The waiter refilled the wine glasses. JayJay went on:

"As horny as I am," she said, "I do love my freedom."

JayJay, beautiful, smart, sexy as hell, and she was a kindred spirit.

"We are also not sleeping together, Covey" (Not yet, I hoped she'd say but she didn't). What I want is to help find Freddie's killer, but by myself, I can't get anywhere. And neither can you if you don't have my assistance."

"Sure, I need all the help I can get, but the sexual tension may be hard to take. But tell me what you told the police."

"Not one motherfucking thing is what I told them— excuse the language."

"No problem. We speak the same language. Did you refuse to talk to them or did they not try?"

"Nah, they didn't know anything about me, but I could have told them stuff."

The waiter brought more wine and more candlewax fell at the candleholder's base (a Luigi added attraction). The food was coming right up. My hunger had almost dissipated. I was enthralled with the woman across the table…

"So, what could you have told them?"

"I have given this a lot of thought…First, Freddie Mae Johnson was no prostitute. She was a businesswoman, a manager. By March 1979, she managed a lot of women, and a few of them were white. Nearly all the clients were white. Freddie Mae Johnson was no street whore like the rumors painted her."

"Right, I knew that she had that as a side job. Bigger operation than I thought."

"After your daddy canned her, she simply stepped up her game and your daddy financed the expansion. He owed her. Let that Irishman help her buy nighties, and other things girls needed."

"What Irishman?"

"That older guy down from Boston who helped on the weekends at the car wash. What was his name, Bill Tool?", asked JayJay.

"Oh, yeah, William O'Toole. I had forgotten all about him."

JayJay continued, "Well, he was more to your daddy than part-time help. He was fixer, muscle, and he knew the guys who wanted the girls. And that is a damned fact. In fact, he came to her house the night she died. I was there!"

"You were? What did he want? What did he say?" I asked.

"I don't know, but I know she left with him."

Bingo, this is my first solid piece of new evidence.

Luigi's food was still great. Not as good as Fio's at the Woodner in D.C., but still good. JayJay had so much to tell me and she had one surprise after another for me as a person. Three hours at the restaurant and she talked ¾ the time. I had so much to unpack, but then two more surprises.

The waiter took my credit card and came back with the receipt.

"Thank you for coming. I hate to intrude, but Ms. Qualls, may I have your autograph?"

"Oh, how kind. Of course," as she wrote her name in a flourish on the slip of paper he handed her. "Thanks."

"Autograph? What else have I missed in my time back here?"

"Like I say, you don't know that much about me. I am an actor as well as a businesswoman. I just played Ophelia at the Globe Theater to pretty good reviews. My bet's that our waiter is gay, an actor, and obviously a perceptive critic."

The Globe. Odessa's recreation of the Bard's theater and where I went to get a modicum of high culture back in the day. It's community theater at its best and it is right on the Odessa College campus. It's still there.

"JayJay, I am dizzy from the wine, from you, and from tonight. We better grab some coffee before I drive back to Odessa," I said.

"Sure, but I made reservations at the Sandalwood Hotel just two blocks from here in case you wanna go there?" she asked.

"You said we weren't going to sleep together!"

JayJay smiled.

"I know, but who said anything about sleeping?"

Chapter 13
Time Management

How could I handle a full load with the three biggest parts of my life: work, the investigation, and a sudden love life, as unconventional as it was turning out to be? JayJay was a remarkable woman and she was more than West Texas blunt.

"No one owns me, Covey. No one owns you. But our being friends means due respect and I expect it."

As a lawyer, I knew a contract when I saw one. But this one looked anything but boilerplate. I could see negotiations, revisions, and maybe even dispute resolution ahead. For my part, I was going to proceed cautiously and listen if there were any codicils or sub-clauses that might modify the object and purpose of the agreement. That is: this ole boy was gonna enjoy the ride but be damned careful.

But about that workload? Now, what would a real boss do? Division of labor! JayJay was going to draw up a list of folks, mostly black, she might talk to. Jack was going to research transportation regs and NAFTA provisions regarding Mexican trucks using Texas roads and highways (an issue fast becoming a political hot potato), and M.A. was interviewing potential candidates for a new associate to join us to backstop Jack and me. "One that speaks Spanish, OK, M.A.?"

I tried to keep my three lives separate from one another, but M.A. is hard not to talk to. Her inquiries about my sleeping and eating habits and my other "job" were, well not quite welcome, but OK. I sorta liked having a West Texas mama lookin' after me. And then there's the fact that she was a computer whiz and generous soul. I needed to find William O'Toole, the man who suddenly appeared as a major player in Freddie's death, and all I had discovered was that he was no longer in Odessa. Who knew if he were alive or dead? Would the internet help? Would M.A. agree to assist me?

"William O'Toole? Wild Bill from Boston?" asked M.A.

"Yes, that's the guy. Do a search?"

"No need. I can start by askin' his daughter, though she hates his guts."

"You know her?" I asked.

"I better. She's my girlfriend. I guess I have to say partner these days," M.A. said.

"What?"

"Don't ask, don't tell, Boss."

Will Odessa wonders never cease?

Chapter 14
As Far as the Eye Can See

Some people think West Texas is desolate. Maybe the vast stretches of desert, scruffy vegetation, and absence of green grass or even short trees inform that view. Or maybe the human additions to the landscape taint the natural beauties of the mesas, the colorful sunrises and sunsets, and not to mention "the stars at night." Tacky and beyond tacky motels, convenience stores, and occasional trailer parks mark parts of the area as not only tasteless but desperately poor. Add garish billboards advertising local businesses, political rants, and the value of billboards themselves and you have perhaps the worst of American consumer culture writ large. As a boy, I always wondered what a lone "Comanch" warrior saw and thought as he rode through this area. He knew the critters and the natural beauty that we overlook, but then he also never knew what lay deep beneath the ground below and how it would change everything above ground.

From the 1920s on, oil brought people to West Texas. They mostly did not revere the land like the Comanches, but they failed even to appreciate it as much as the ranchers who settled there in the late 19th century. They came to conquer and generate personal wealth. That they did and more. And the people today, what we might call the "Children of the Crude"? They value their families, their status, their wealth, but what they think of the land around them or the larger environment ranges from the instrumental to the apathetic, to the hostile. There are some, but very few, "tree huggers." I guess that is because there are very few trees to begin with. And the children of the Children? They seem fixated on the Music City Mall, football, and whatever gadget or obsession can pass their time of day before they "can get out of this damned place." At least until they can get away long enough to miss it.

These musings rattled around my brain as I sat parked on Old Crane Highway one Sunday morning across from the place where the roughnecks found Freddie Mae. It was a curious place to find her both because there was no reason for her to be there and because the property had a unique history. Once the Carleton ranching family owned everything from the highway to as far as the eye could see out in the desert. Over time, it stopped being a working ranch as the family sold oil leases here and there but at some point old man Carleton had enough money and he had had his fill of "roughnecks." He refused to sell any more land to the Huckabee Drilling Company and he turned about five acres and the barn into a rent-a-pony, rent-a-horse site for 1960s teens to relive the Cowboy ways by riding horses for an hour at a time. It made money but not oil money. I was one of the occasional riders. Jack had reminded me of those fun days when I originally told him the details of Freddie's death. Now the barn stood empty and decrepit. Carleton's two "boys" sold everything up to the barn to Huckabee as soon as the old man died. I had two concerns now. How did Freddie end up here and why did the boys, Delbert, Jr., and Aaron, not simply sell the whole lot? Surely, the barn was of no use to anyone and yet there it stood.

As I drove away to go to Friendship to meet JayJay and then catch lunch at Underwood's BBQ, I made a mental note to look into the land sales between Carleton and Huckabee and to track down where the two Carleton boys had ended up. Something didn't smell quite right on Old Crane Highway and it wasn't just the natural gas.

Chapter 15
Settling Down?

Over a year in the Big O and I still lived in the temporary motel suites that I thought I'd stay in for a couple of months. Jencks and Associates was a real thing. JayJay and I loved being with each other and it was a close to a cross between a real relationship and "friends with benefits" as you could imagine. I was forever flying to D.C., attending NTSB hearings in Austin and elsewhere or popping over to Abilene to visit Mr. Franklin. She worked hard at Sewell's, taught an actors' class for kids at the Globe and disappeared for a few days at a time. She belonged to Odessa. I did not ask questions about where she disappeared to and she did not ask about D.C.

JayJay lived on the south side, a place most white Odessans knew nothing about. Odessa's 6,000 black residents had their own town with their own stores, barbershops, salons, restaurants, like Fat's in the old days, and especially churches. There were three Baptist churches and one Methodist AME church. I heard no one call it the Hood. Everyone called it the "Flats" and it was still a real community even though it had changed some from its early 50s/60s start. In those days everyone was poor, minimum wage jobs, or worse, for those who had work, and nowadays some people's fortunes had improved, like JayJay's, and some had declined as recessions, drugs, and competition for jobs with Mexicans and Mexican-Americans heated up. The neighborhoods did have some small houses, some dreary apartments, and one fairly nice place called The Manor. The

Manor was an apartment one block north of Friendship Baptist and it's where JayJay lived. It was nice and JayJay's small one-bedroom with a fairly modern kitchen, living room, and study "nook" was so neat and proper I felt my very presence messed it up a bit.

By the 90s inter-racial dating was not unknown in Odessa. Still, some folks on both sides of the tracks were less than accepting. JayJay, ever practical, told me to assume some less than warm receptions. If anyone said anything directly to her, she was ready with a "Mind your own damned business," and that usually worked. But she said, that despite her a good standing on the south side, there were still folks who did not like her dating a white guy, did not like her working at Sewell's, and did not like her looks.

"What, your looks? Pure jealousy, I said."

"No, Liberal Boy, I am too black, too African, for some people. Didn't you ever see *School Daze*?"

"Yes, but I'll be switched. I never thought you…"

"Yes, me, but I live a lot in the white world and to them black is black, so they either tolerate me or they don't. I just don't worry about it. Besides, it's true that a person usually has just a small number of friends anyway and I have got some really good ones on both sides of the tracks."

The last line of the Serenity Prayer is "And accept (the things) that I cannot change."

Despite all she had been through in life I was being to think that JayJay was the answer to that prayer and maybe to mine.

"Is this what love feels like?" I wondered.

Chapter 16
Surprise, Surprise

Maybe it was the idea of taking JayJay to a motel on occasion or maybe it was a sense that it was time to accept the fact that I was beginning to like life in Odessa, but suddenly I felt that I need to buy a house. In. D.C., hotels for me meant clandestine liaisons for purposes of needy sex. While the need was still there, Odessa was not D.C. and JayJay was not a temporary hook up. I started thinking about putting down roots in West Texas. Oh, I still did not like the political hysteria in town about the Clintons or the sandstorms that covered everything inside and out with dust, but in fact, Odessans are, to your face, about the nicest people on earth. Truth is, no white person, had ever complained to me about JayJay, so my worry about how I would defend my honor or hers seemed just irrelevant. Besides, she did not need a white savior, and more people appeared to know and like her every day. So this is how my mind works; I needed to become more respectable and what's says respectable more than a home purchase?

Santa Rita Drive. This had always been my idea of settled Odessa. Nice but not gigantic homes on well-kept streets and even some trees, situated on the west side on the Odessa High School part of town, not on the east side where my Permian is and where I grew up. I liked "owning" both sides of town, being invested in the south side, and having a home fairly close to the office. I always want an office I can walk to and did so even in D.C. Commuting is just not my thing.

I do like to drive, though. I like to drive, listen to George Jones, and think. My thoughts mostly centered on JayJay, work, and what to do next about the investigation. I satisfied myself that by renting rather buying furniture I could still lay claim to vagabond ways, but in other parts of my life, I had essentially the same question: where is this going? On Freddie's case, I was really stumped. JayJay's inquiries had turned up little new except that Freddie had in fact angered some of the church ladies on the south side a good bit by expanding her operation, but I still knew nothing about whether Bill O'Toole was more than a one-time fixer for Freddie, whether the location of her death was significant, or whether some random factor, or person, would pop up to lead me in a different direction. The land sales were all in order. But one of my old Political Science professors at Austin College always said, "Expect the unexpected."

Also unexpected was what M.A. said after I moved into Santa Rita.

"Covey, we need to have a house-warming party!"

That's when it struck me. All this time since Jencks and Associates started and I have never met M.A.'s Beth, Erica's Martin, or the new guy, Alberto Garza's Juanita. And Jack's Dana? Other than talking to her on the phone a couple of times, I have not laid eyes on one of my old friends since moving back to town. What kind of person am I? My house and Alberto's coming on board made a party a good idea. He was the young 'un in the office. Not two years out of Tech law school, preceded by his attendance at the University of Texas at El Paso; he was born and bred in Odessa and his hiring makes Jencks look more and more

72

like the real Odessa. He knew everyone, and he had been the Drum Major at OHS back in high school. His open and happy nature changed the office dramatically, but it was lucky I was almost never there because Lee Street was getting crowded. It was time to celebrate and grow closer.

My fear was that I was not up to it. I watched Mary Tyler Moore in the 70s and I figured that I would be every bit as terrible as she at giving a party. So, I didn't. Not in Odessa; not in College; and never after I started working. I confided this deep dark secret to M.A. and she was unmoved by its pathos.

"Bull shit, Boss. All you need for a West Texas party are nachos and beer. We'll do the rest. Beth and I will even stay to help clean up."

Party at my house.

Chapter 17
And Then There's This

Tacos, guacamole, cold beer and sopapillas actually kept things moving at my place. Alberto brought his trumpet and damned if he could not play that thing. We could not resist asking him to play the Mexican dirge John Wayne said the Mexican army played before attacking the Alamo, *Deguello*, even if it meant sure death for all the Texicans. Not so secretly Texans love that haunting music. But who stole the show that night? M.A.'s Beth. She swapped stories and told tales with the best. Her stories of growing up in the "real North" shattered stereotypes. South Boston's racism, girl fights in the schoolyard, and Irish/Italian rivalries beat about anything we had ever heard. She told all in a loud voice and laughed heartedly when saying something like "if it weren't for the nuns, I'd probably been a gangster like my daddy."

Wild Bill O'Toole. My daddy's buddy. The last person as far as I know who saw Freddie the night she died. We asked about what exactly his criminal activities entailed but Beth knew few specifics.

"Other than overseeing a prostitution ring," she laughed. "I didn't know much he did. I do know that's why we ended up in the desert."

Golly.

"How did you know about that?" I asked.

"Well, I heard a screaming match between him and mama. Evidently, he had sampled the services and she found out. They never knew I knew, but I always assumed it's why we went to the end of the earth to get away from something."

After a while, the others found at least two dancers among the celebrants-JayJay and Jack (I stayed quiet, 'cause this boy can dance). Everyone then tried to get those two to show them how to dance the Mash Potatoes, a dance both acquired in high school and the others had never heard of. Jack, agile as a teenager, could hit it and, well JayJay, was so cool she was doubly hot. She got a laugh every time she told Jack "you're good for a white boy." A good night for disposing of stereotypes.

As they moved on to the Twist and the Jitterbug, I noticed Beth head for...the bathroom, no kitchen. I followed in a minute.

"Beth, thanks for coming. Those are wild stories."

"Nothing but the truth, counselor."

"I did not know you back in the day. In fact, I did not even know *of* you."

"Yeah, that's because the move here did not solve Bill's and Marian's marital issues. They split, and I stayed with mom."

"Did he fall back into his old ways?" I asked.

"Could be, but the biggest issue was his shenanigans at the American Legion and the bad crowd that he hung out with there," she said.

"Oh, do tell."

Chapter 18
Heroes and Zeros

Like a lot of towns, especially in the south, Odessa honors its vets. Odessa has had many, including my dad and Beth's dad. I am one myself and the farther away I get from service the more I understand its importance. As a teenager, I also heard the story of Marvin "Rex" Young, who fought and died in Viet Nam. Before dying in a horrific shootout with the Viet Cong, he led his men on the ground and was a fierce warrior in protecting his unit. Eventually, he was awarded the Congressional Medal of Honor. Think what you will about Viet Nam or war itself, but Rex put service above self in Viet Nam and lost his life for it. You see, I knew all about Rex Young. I loved playing Little League and Pony League baseball games in Odessa in the lazy summers of the 60s and 70s. As fate would have it, my coach in each league also coached Rex Young. He became my unmet role model. He was a happy guy, a funny guy, a scrappy guy, and one hell of a leader. Others may have chosen football heroes to hope to emulate, but I chose Rex Young.

The American Legion, out east on Eighth Street towards Midland, also played in my family history. My dad was a member and he was "over at the Legion Hall" a lot. Occasionally there were family events there and though rarely was my whole family together, when we were, it was often at American Legion-hosted parties or celebrations. Once at ten, I entered and excelled in a shooting contest that resulted in my winning a huge Thanksgiving Turkey. In the final three shots, I got two bull's eyes and another near bull's eye at 50 yards. I beat adults and I beat other kids, but what I remember most is the turkey my mom cooked up for Thanksgiving at one of the few holiday meals my dad ever attended.

Odessans cheer for vets and celebrate them as few other communities do. Sometimes they take it too far as they embrace the likes of Oliver North as a true patriot who simply did what's right and damn the political torpedoes. As a lawyer and a patriot, to me, he was a rogue ideologue who broke the law, subverted the Constitution, and thumbed his nose at Democracy during the Iran Contra Affair in the 80s. I did not have much company on this view in the Big O.

But Bill O'Toole's Legion crowd rose neither to the level of legitimate heroes nor to the glory of wrong-headed patriots. That they were vets is mere coincidence and the Legion Hall is simply where they met. And drank. And schemed. And hatched a plan to feed men's libidos for fun and profit. All Beth really knew was that they rented the Legion Hall, charged the fellas $50 a head, hired strippers, and threw a drunken party at which more than one Legionnaire sexually penetrated more than one stripper in public--to the whistles and catcalls of all the other attendees.

The Legion brass found out about the party and laid the hammer down. They summarily banned Bill and his cohorts from the Hall and they notified their wives and families that they had been dishonorably discharged from the American Legion (which is not a thing, but they liked the sound of it).

That is how Bill O'Toole's last humiliation played out. Beth had no idea what happened to his two other accomplices for the Legion party: Delbert and Aaron Carleton, the owners of the barn where Freddie had died.

Chapter 19
No Rest for the Wicked

Reluctantly I came to the conclusion that I had to go to Monahan's, Texas. Monahans is 35, or so, miles southwest of Odessa and less than half as big. It is the home of the Monahans' Sand Hills where, as teenagers, we played "search party" and ran up and down the dunes wearing leg weights to get in shape for football. "Search party" was great fun since it meant one group of boys headed for Monahans 30 minutes before another group would follow behind and track them through the sand hills as best they could. Once Jack, as a member of the searchers, surprised another set of boys from Monahans as he was looking for me and my other Permian buddies. The Monahans boys had words for the Permian boy out there seemingly alone and one yelled the inevitable insult often shared by West Texas hotheads, "You come from Odessa? All's they have in Odessa is steers and queers!" Jack knocked him down with one punch and turned to the other and said, "Come on, Boy, I got one for you, too." We laughed hysterically as Jack recounted how that boy ran up a sand hill as fast as he could, falling and swearing every other step.

But I digress.

I didn't drive over to Monahans for old time's sake. I went there to talk to Frank Jencks, my one and only old man. I had been known to refer to him as "Darth Vader of the Desert." This was the SOB who cheated on my mom, ran me down in every way, and fired Freddie Mae. He also played fast and loose in business matters and cut every corner and took every unfair advantage of every customer and every business partner he possibly could. He smoked two packs of cigarettes a day, started drinking before noon most days, and played poker at the Legion Hall to mid-night or later several times a week. He refused to help me pay for college and he never came to any of my ball games, graduations, or birthday parties. He once slapped a Mexican girl at the car wash for "looking at him funny." He was my daddy.

He ended up at the Rest Assured Nursing Home in Monahans because he wanted no one in Odessa ever to see him down and out. The former Car Wash King had his pride. I had very little to do with him after I left Odessa, but I did once fly back the summer of 1989 to take him to Houston's M.D. Anderson Hospital where they were attempting to treat his throat and lung cancer that he had honestly acquired from Camels' unfiltered cigarettes. M.D. Anderson had cut out his larynx but decided not to subject his lungs to chemo or operate on his heart because they guessed he was too weak to survive any of it. I took him back to a small Odessa apartment where his girlfriend of the hour, Elsie Jo Hooper, took care of him in hopes of coming into some money for herself. As a former nurse, she could at least make him comfortable as she somehow got access to morphine pills. But in 1991, Frank figured out how to qualify for Medicaid, get rid of Elsie, and get out of Odessa. I have no idea how he got over to Monahans physically, but I was hoping I would never see him or Elsie Jo Hogwaller (my cruel "Oh, Brother Where Art Thou" name for Ms. Hooper) ever again. I assumed that he would die soon, but, no, he was too ornery for that.

But as luck would have it, I need to talk to Frank about some of the things we had turned up. Probably he knew about Bill O'Toole's dealings with Freddie and maybe even with the Carleton Brothers. I figured he was one of the men at the strip party and he may have also known about what those idiots had done at the barn. My guess was something pretty bad. Going to see Frank, I knew there was good news and bad news waiting. The good news was that the folks at Rest Assured told me that, despite everything, Frank's mind was pretty sharp and he liked to talk about his car wash days to anyone who took the time to read his lips and hear his whisperings. He had no truck with a mechanical voice box since it made him sound like a robot. The bad news was that he still hated me and talked every day about how I had abandoned him. He was right about that.

Finding Rest Assured was easy. It was right off of Interstate 20 and right behind the Dairy Queen. Monahans made Odessa look like Las Vegas, especially that part of town. Dilapidated houses, debris from the highway, rusted pipe fences, and scruffy grass and ugly sand and dirt everywhere. But nothing prepared me for walking into Rest Assured. The smell of shit hit me two steps into the place and the nurse on duty was as old as the sand hills and literally had no teeth. I could not understand a word she said and I wanted to walk away seconds after I walked in. Then I saw Frank being wheeled my way and I knew I had to say something.

"Hello, Daddy. They taking good care of you here?"

He whispered something that I could not hear, but maybe I could not comprehend it because all I could focus on was the mucus bubbling from the hole in his throat. Damn, I wanted out of that place. Overwhelming guilt also hit me. I had abandoned him and now that I had seen him and this place, how could I leave him? Maybe I had better reconsider it.

"Look who the mangy cat dragged in," is what he said.

"Yep, nice to see you too," I managed to respond.

"They tell me you came back to Odessa."

"I did. Opened up a law practice," I said.

"Fucking lawyer! I should have guessed."

Niceties aside, we did get to visit. The thing about Frank was that he still loved to talk. I wheeled him back to his private room that did not smell as bad as some and did not seem as depressing as the outer lobby. "I am leaving him here" came to my mind. And I hope I never come back.

"You got the money?" he asked.

"Yes, I got it."

"Give it back!" he yelled to the top of his whisper.

"OK, I will as soon as you get out of here," I replied with a slight grin.

"That will be next week."

"Sure, OK, give me a ring."

He actually smiled. Both of us knew he was not getting out. My dad back in the day was 6'0' tall, weighed 140 pounds, had jet black hair, and wore cool dark shades. My mom and other women compared him to Clark Gable. I, on the other hand, was 5"9", 170 pounds, and had a flat top head of dull brown hair. Today, I had gained 10 pounds, let my hair grow longer, but was basically the same, but older, guy. Before me, Frank looked shriveled, maybe 100 pounds, had thinning gray hair, and did I mention the hole in his throat? He looked every bit a dying man.

I could not be direct with Frank. He was not a true West Texan. As soon as I showed my hand, he would want to figure an angle or tell a tale.

Ten minutes into our conversation and after reminding him that Frank's No. 2 Car Wash was no longer standing and that our old house on Patton Street had fallen on hard times, I casually mentioned that I had met Bill O'Toole's daughter. That hit his last nerve.

"Bill O'Toole? That Irish SOB. Who cares if he has a daughter?" Daddy asked.

For the next hour, Frank spun a tale of betrayal and hurt feelings. The gist of it was that Bill left Frank's employ and started an "operation" with two "fellers" who had more money than sense. It had to do with Mexico, young girls, and sicko businessmen. While I was fascinated to discover that my dad had yet unrevealed ethical boundaries, I wanted to know more. So, these guys were trafficking women? How? Was Freddie somehow involved? Were they ever caught? Did Freddie's death play a part of it?

"Daddy, I never heard or read anything about this. Forgive the question, but were you involved?"

"Shit, no, but I loaned O'Toole $3,000 and all he did was pay me back with a little interest. He said his runnin' buddies didn't want any more partners. I told that Irish bastard to get lost."

Forget what I said about ethical boundaries.

83

Chapter 20
Muscle Man

JayJay was nonplussed.

"Covey, this is worse than I thought. Wild sex parties and even prostitution are bad, but this? Bringing girls in from Mexico? Probably under-aged girls at that? I can't see Freddie being mixed up in any of this. Bill yes, but Freddie no."

"I can't either, but she did manage women. I can't let my mind go there."

"Well, I do know something about this. Freddie took care of the women who worked for her. She bought condoms for them. She helped them if abusive men followed them. She made sure they were safe and as healthy as they could be. Thankfully, that was in the days when weed was the drug of choice. Funny thing I now remember. The women's name for Freddie was 'Mama Fish'. She took care of them. There were no children involved."

"Who was her muscle?"

"What do you mean?" she asked.

I replied, "Well, who physically protected her 'workers'? Who would she have gotten to cut off your daddy's dick? She had to have a tough guy or two and it could not have been just Wild Bill."

"You are right about protection, but I can figure who it was. That had to be Willie Gumble."

"Gumble? The boxer?"

"I forgot that he boxed sometimes, but he was the baddest man on the south side. That scar up the side of his face was a sign. As in you should've seen the other guy—if you could only find the pieces."

"Please tell me that he doesn't still live here, so I don't have to talk to him," I said.

"Oh, he still lives here, but you ain't talkin' to him."

"No?"

"Let's just say that his racial attitudes are pretty far south of Martin Luther King's. I will talk to him," she asserted.

"You sure? If he knows you date a white man…?"

"Yeah, yeah. He won't like it, but he loved Freddie and back then he surely loved me. I am not worried."

"OK, I will worry for both of us. If he is so bad, might he have killed Freddie?" I asked.

"I don't think so, but he might just kill you for suggesting it."

Gulp.

Willie Gumble was now in his late 40s. He was still a massive person. Over 6 feet tall, closer to 240 pounds than one or two biscuits, and he obviously still worked out-a lot. In his 20s he had been a US Ranger. Another vet, and a successful businessman. That is, he made money. These days, curiously enough, he occasionally rode shotgun for truckers going into and out of Juarez, Mexico. He was glad to see JayJay.

"Hey there, Girl. You grew up real nice. You still working for Sewell's over on 8th?"

JayJay was glad that was his rap to start out. I did not come up and she was able to ask Willie what she needed. She didn't know exactly how to pose the question, so she just said it:

"Back in the day, Mr. Willie, when you worked with Ms. Freddie, did she ever help white men bring Mexican girls into Odessa?"

"God damn, JayJay, you knew about that?" Willie asked.

JayJay's heart sunk. "I just found out about it."

JayJay and Willie were meeting at "Cousin's Mechanics," a collision repair shop three blocks from Dixie. Two black lawn chairs next to the building were well worn but they afforded privacy and, being on the west side of the building, protection from the rising sun. The shop was open but there were no loud noises coming from inside.

"Miss Freddie learnt about that operation not too long before she died," said Willie. "She was furious because that white man, Wild Bill they called him, who had helped her some, was getting involved with it too."

"Did she ask you to, ummm, talk to Wild Bill?" JayJay inquired.

"No, she talked to him her own damn self. You know he was tappin' that shit?"

"Freddie and Wild Bill?" was JayJay's stunned response.

"Oh, yeah, that's why that car wash man let her go? He thought Freddie was his woman, but Freddie don't belong to no man."

"I know that, but if she was furious, could she make him stop bringing those girls in?" JayJay asked.

"I know she was gonna try to convince him, but Cleon killed her before she could get it done."

"You think Cleon did it?"

"I ain't sure, but I know that story about him passin' out at Fat's is a damn lie. I saw his sorry ass drive away that night my own damn self. I was takin' a piss aside the building and I seen him. He a'int never tole the truth about that night even if he and Jesus are close these days," Willie said.

"But Cleon is back in town?" she asked.

"Oh, I know what you mean? Did I go over and hurt that nigger?"

"I guess, yes, that's what I mean."

"I got him beat up real good when he was in Huntsville and they broke him down. He still say he didn't kill Freddie. I don't believe him, but I don't know for sure. Reverend Leroy axed me not to hurt Cleon no more onct he come back to Odessa, so I let it go. How come you askin' about all this now?" Willie asked.

"Well, a friend and I are looking into Freddie's death…"

"OK then, you tell that White Boy lawyer friend that if he needs anything, I will help for a small fee. Freddie Mae Johnson was the best person I ever knew. And tell him to treat you good 'cause you are second on that list."

She was busted but also relieved. Willie knew more than he let on, sure, but now we knew. He was on our side. And he was dangerous.

Chapter 21
Talk About Mixed Feelings

People in Odessa came to Jencks and Associates, I am sure, because we are great lawyers and nice people. Our lower prices may also have helped, but with M.A.'s experience and Alberto's willingness to work, we did a great job for our "little" clients. We passed on nothing-wills, real estate, personal injury, any kind of contracts. Now I am not saying we had lots of work in each category, but M.A. could line it up and Alberto could knock it down. Either Jack or I reviewed every case. Ninety per cent of the time we settled, but almost always to our client's advantage. Meanwhile, Jack and I helped Ranger and its partner hauling companies. The latest thing was to assist them in getting sub-contract jobs from larger trucking companies in Dallas and San Antonio as NAFTA kept increasing the demand. Connections from Austin College, Tech Law, or UT Law always came in handy, as did Permian football.

In mid-October, Jack and I even went to Ratliff Stadium (capacity 20,000) to watch Mojo beat down OHS 22-6 for their 28th win in a row over the scrappy but hapless Bronchos (I swear that's how they spell it). Jack and I sat on the OHS side the first half and Permian's the second half. Both of us remarked that we probably could not make this Permian team as players. Later they made it to the State semi-finals and lost to another legendary team, the Plano Wildcats, 0-10. This is about like the Yankees losing to the Rex Sox in the American League title game, or perhaps vice versa. Truth be known, this game was another step toward settling back into Odessa. Jencks and Associates took out ads in both schools' game programs which in Odessa is full out "going public." More than once a Permian backer recognized Jack and one time an old teacher of mine even recalled my exploits in making tackles on kick-offs inside the 20-yard line. As a knowledgeable fan, he remarked, "Field position, field position! Field position wins games." Could I just go ahead and accept credit for all eight of our wins? Funny, I was almost sucked back into thinking that high school football was life itself. Or at least important.

Just as I was feeling warm and fuzzy towards Odessa, Jack and I returned to the very crowded Ratliff parking to find my car with four flat tires and a not so welcoming message tucked underneath the driver's side windshield wiper: "Go back north, nigger lover!" The genius had written it in his own hand, but the vandalism and the advice were stark warnings. Triple A took care of the car eventually, but I now had another factor to juggle in my already complicated life. Of course, this was garden variety racism, so my concerns were whether it posed any danger to JayJay or me and whether or not it in anyway related to our Freddie investigation. I leaned toward just the first conclusion since our inquiries into Freddie's death had been done almost exclusively in the black community. But one never knows, do one?

I decided to report the incident to the Police. Well, not exactly to the police, but to a certain policeman, Dan Gladstone. There may have been more than one aggressive racist in town, but this one I knew and this one had been involved in Freddie's case. Moreover, he was not smart enough to hide his guilt, if any.

I also told JayJay about the note and I told her about my plan.

"Well, it took longer to happen than I thought it would. I've already had friends on the south side ask me if we knew what we're doin'."

"We agree that we do, right?" I asked.

"Why would you ask that?"

"Oh, I don't mean anything by it," I asserted.

"Walk away any time you like!"

"Hold on now. Don't go there. I know what I am doin' and I am not walkin' away," I replied.

"Why not? It may be gettin' dangerous."

"I'd walk away from Odessa or from the investigation before I walked away from you," I said.

"Really?"

"Damn straight. You want me to say it?" I asked.

"Yes, I guess I do."

"JayJay, I love you. Through thick and thin. In Texas or out."

"I love you, too, Covey Jencks. Now let's find out where we stand with these rednecks."

Chapter 22
Old Times Not Forgotten

I grew up hearing Biblical and secular excuses for racism. Something about a cursed strain of persons from Cain's loins, though of course black people came first in the evolution of things. I heard more than one person say "I don't have any prejudices against black folks. It's just their habits I can't stand." Habits, they said, like being lazy, cowardly, stupid, and lusting after white women. Habits like being poor and desperate. And many, many times I heard that blacks were afraid of a man's game like football. These things were "common knowledge" and as much as we wanted to love them as equals per our Christian duty, they just weren't up to the rigors of civilized society. But, of course, there were good ones (docile) and bad ones (uppity). As a child and as a teenager, this is what I heard from many white Odessans. I am sure some disagreed, but I never heard from them. Oh, but I did hear references to Martin Luther Coon a great deal.

Since I worked with black folks at my dad's car wash, they were my co-workers and just about every day associates. Empirical observation showed me smart people, hard-working people, principled people, and brave people. I also met some others, white and black, who did not pass the decency or the smart test. I also met and overheard many white men who lusted after black women. I got to figuring that the lust thing just had no color line. My own father saw everything I saw at the car wash, but he managed to hold on to his racism all the way to the nursing home.

Dan Gladstone was working on his own lifetime of hatred. I knew this because I had seen it in action. The very first day I ever saw him, I drove up to his house and he was taking a strap to my classmate and then friend, Bo Gladstone. It turned out that Bo had allowed a black man to "disrespect" him. That is, the man did not call Bo "sir" as he filled Bo's motor scooter at a gas station over on 2nd street. Bo and I were both 13 at the time and Dan was 30, a veteran, and a man. He was angry and not too bright. And he was easy to provoke. Some called him troubled.

"Dan, I remember back when I was in junior high you told Bo and me that blacks were too undisciplined to play ball. How did that prediction work out?"

I had asked Dan to meet me at Music City Mall in hopes of reigning in his temper. Sitting on a bench between Burger King and a record store might help. He was out of uniform.

"Well, my nephew plays with them. Mostly they cheat at the game and pretend to be hurt in practice. The coaches let them get away with murder," Dan said.

"Uh huh, being bigger, faster and stronger also helps, huh?

"What do you want, Jencks?" he asked.

I handed him the terrorist note.

"Did you write this?"

He read it very slowly and then chuckled at the end.

"Heh, heh, I guess if the shoe fits, it makes sense. No, I did not write it. Did you?" Dan asked.

92

"Of course not. I will re-write it in my hand if you will do the same."

"Bull shit, Jencks. You can't just go around accusing folks of things and demanding they do what you say."

"OK, how about you just write your name?"

"How about if you eat shit and die?"

"Let's say you didn't write this. Let's say I just bring it in and ask what the police department can do about it. What kind of answer will I get?" I asked.

"Oh, I dunno. Like it would not be a priority to find who done it and it'd be hard to find that person anyway. It is not a real threat and I guess it's just some high school kid actin' out."

"Yeah, I figured. Here's how I see it. I am staying in Odessa. I am seeing who I want to see. And I am protecting myself and her. No one should doubt that," I explained.

"That's right. Stir things up. Typical agitator. I guess it'd be my job to protect you if it came to that, but, come the time, sure hope I don't have four flat tires."

"Thanks for helping me out, Dan. You are every bit as sharp now as you were back in the day. Say hey to Bo for me."

Chapter 23
The Human Condition

"Two things, JayJay. He did it or knows who did it. But the other thing is I don't think he was trying to scare me off the investigation."

"Why's that?" she asked.

"When we played poker me as a teenager and him as an older man, he always gave his hand away. This time he tipped his hand on the flat tires but in no way, subtle or not, did he warn me off looking for Freddie's killer. He either knows about it and doesn't care, or he doesn't know."

"You worried about what comes next? What he might do to you or me?"

"Not really. He got my message. He figures I am on to him and that if anything happens, he will be suspect. That should deter him," I asserted.

"That may be an unexamined assumption. Are others in on it?"

"I think he is a rogue actor. I doubt it's a police conspiracy," I said.

"Oh, the old saying that racism 'is just in part of the system. It is not the system'," she asserted.

"There has to be a difference in racisms. Sometimes it will be just prejudice and stupid assumptions and sometimes it will be violent and dangerous. Probably the vast majority here just shutter and whisper when they see us. I am acting on the assumption that most people, even the cops, just live with prejudice and don't resort to KKK terrorism. You know, some racism bubbles up over the top and some is simply on permanent low reserve. Or do you wanna pack up and head to Austin? "

"Nah, I am used to this place. Besides we have not yet driven the property values down on Santa Rita far enough for my cousins to move in. Let's stay a while," she concluded.

Chapter 24
Learning from History

When I was a boy in elementary school and junior high, I loved the history I was taught. Egypt came up, Mesopotamia came up, the United States, especially the "War Between the States," came up, and crushingly boring Texas History came up. Only the Alamo and the Battle of San Jacinto ever caught my attention. Curiously, no one ever mentioned much about West Texas history specifically. The tens of thousands of people from all over these United States who flooded into West Texas in the 1950s to make Odessa the fastest growing town in America; who set roughneck Odessa off against corporate Midland; and who attracted not one but two U.S. presidents, numbers 41 and 43, knew next to nothing about Apaches, Comanches, Mexican bandits, and turf wars between cattle ranchers and sheepherders. They did not and could not relate to the isolation of the small outposts of white people who came west, fought the Indians, and relied on US Government inducements and Texas Rangers' protection to settle the land and to pacify the indigenous peoples. Their harsh reality and their pioneer ways were celebrated with some tall tales, a few street names, and complete reverence for the Texas Rangers, but we never learned the details, not even those pertaining to the white people. There were families here and there who preserved the legacy of those times with oral traditions, but most of us unwashed newcomers were steeped in ignorance, and there were a hell of a lot more of us than of them. Watching *The Searchers* or even *Giant* just wasn't enough.

By my time, we knew that the Scarbauer family over in Midland and the Parker family in Odessa were royalty and we knew Odessa had had ranchers after 1881, but most of them turned to oil after the 1920s. Clarence Carleton once worked for Clarence Scarbauer, but he started his own place in 1900 just outside Odessa, and his son, Delbert, Sr. maintained it through cattle, oil, and downtown investment through the 60s. Delbert's two boys, Delbert, Jr. and slightly younger Aaron, could not really identify themselves as ranchers or oilmen even if they did affect the look with boots, blue jeans, and Cowboy hats. By the time they were teenagers in the late 50s, such garb was more curious than custom and even rodeos at the Ector County Coliseum drew far fewer folks than either the annual oil shows or the state meetings of the John Birch Society.

But Delbert and Aaron did have an identity. They were the almost rich kids who were neither very smart nor at all athletic. They were the boys who hung out a lot at Day's Drive Inn on 8th and drove one hot car. It was a "cherry red" '55 Chevy with a '60 Corvette engine. Boys said it looked good, sounded good, and ran "real good." The 1950s car culture that thrived in Odessa at places like Day's and Tommy's Drive Inn is now permanently enshrined in 1950s Odessa then-teenage males' memories and Delbert and Aaron tried to sustain it deep into the 60s through "on the edge of town" drag races at night. I saw one of these as a kid and though it scared me to death, I had to admit "the Red" was really fast and Delbert seemed an expert driver. One stunt they also pulled with "Red" pretty much ended their "derring-do" and caused a family ruckus of major proportions. That incident now seemed worthy of review in light of what I was finding out about Freddie's 1979 death. It had to do with a little game the boys called "nigger knocking."

The boys would load up the Red with three friends in the back seat and drive to the south side. The idea was to drive down Old Dixie on the south side and catch an inattentive black man walking on the street. Delbert would move the car over to the right side of the street where Aaron would lean out of the open passenger while wielding a broom handle and whack the man in the back of the head as Delbert sped off. Evidently, they had pulled off this little stunt successfully at least once before but on this one occasion, the man turned at exactly the right time, grabbed the broom handle with his left hand and yanked Aaron by the shirt onto the street with his right hand. Delbert, showing no courage but some good sense, zoomed away in a deft U-turn that took him back over the tracks and just a few blocks to the police station where he excitedly informed the cops that Aaron had been attacked. The cops jumped into their cars and rushed to where Aaron had been manhandled only to find the boy walking back toward them wearing only his "tighty whiteys." Whoever "attacked" Aaron was nowhere to be found and Aaron reckoned that he could not identify the perp on that day or any other.

The truth is that both sides of the tracks got a huge laugh at the boys' expense, but their daddy found it less than amusing. Willie Gumble also did not think it funny, but his decision not to beat the scrawny kid into a pulp probably saved him jail time. The story spread around the teenage population of Odessa like wildfire and no detail was spared. The Carletons were brutally mocked.

Years later I made a mental note that the racism in the Carleton family occasionally bubbled over into incomprehensively stupid violence. That might be relevant information.

Chapter 25
Going Public

In D.C. I dreamed of the day that I would crack the Freddie case. As I walked southwest on New Hampshire Avenue towards DuPont Circle on my way to K. St., I imagined how it would play out. Working alone I'd find the clues, question the suspects, pursue the villains, and unveil, no doubt, a vast conspiracy involving corrupt political leaders or perhaps the CEO of the largest oil company on the planet. What? Have I never seen a movie or read a mystery novel? In most, the protagonist should just skip all the hard sleuthing and simply barge into to the office most prestigious person in the story and shout "J'accuse!" Freshman French aside, the real case was turning out just a bit differently. No corrupt mayors, ambitious police chiefs, or oil barons were anywhere to be seen. All we had were spoiled almost-rich boys, a shabby Boston lowlife, and a now chastened ex-con whose story may or may not hold up. More importantly, it was getting harder and harder to envision how I, I mean we, could go much further without more help or more visibility from white Odessa. Now that might be the tricky bit.

JayJay called it "going white." True, Jack, M.A., and Beth knew what we were up to, but they were white family. How could we widen our scope but still stay under the radar? I did not want unnecessary attention for the firm nor did I want to alert any possible conspirators.

Time for another house party.

It was a low-key affair this time but all were present. Jencks and related family were all in our comfortable living room. Jack even got my end of the brown leather couch next to the end table with the lamp and the TV remote. I stood as the others arranged themselves for story time. JayJay had the Margaritas ready. She grabbed a spot on the floor next to the ottoman by the big chair where M.A. settled in. The others used chairs from the living room and kitchen. I felt like Eisenhower on the eve of D-Day.

I spun the tale and only Beth made a sound. When Wild Bill's role unfolded, she exclaimed, "Big fucking surprise!" Juanita turned bright red from the profanity. Finally, I wrapped up where we stood.

Jack asked the obvious:

"OK, why this meeting? Why us? You know better than to involve the firm."

JayJay pointed at him and nodded yes. I also nodded.

"Right," I said. "But I need your collective wisdom on some things. I think we need to find a knowledgeable insider who is willing to talk to us on the down low about what we know that is not public knowledge. I am thinking a cop or newspaper person. Anyone know a plucky news lady or deeply troubled, soon-to-be-retired detective?"

"To do what?" asked Erica.

"I'd like to know what they know about Freddie's murder but didn't tell or pursue."

"M.A., you have any ideas?"

Back and forth we went, and I honestly did not pay attention to who was talking and who was not. I asked about newspaper contacts at the *Odessa American, Midland*

101

Reporter, and even the *Monahans News*. We eliminated the police pretty quickly.

"Finally, Alberto said, "Hey, boss, we are here, too."

"Excuse me?" I asked.

"No offense, or maybe a little, but you are only mentioning white papers and white persons."

Fool that I am I turned to JayJay. Sagacious person she is, she said, "Not black, Liberal Boy, brown!"

"Oh! Alberto, tell me. What have I missed?"

"Well, not to put too fine a point, but the second largest community in Odessa and the fastest growing."

"Que Mongo! Idiot!" I said to myself.

"So, there is a Spanish language newspaper and it serves the south side Mexicans and Mexican-Americans?"

"Si."

"And it's been around a long time?"

"Claro"

"And, idiot that I am, we know the editor?"

"No," he said.

"No?"

"The owner."

"Tell me."

He looked at Erica.

"Erica's abuella."

It's *El Diario* founded in 1956 and Larraine Garza, Erica's grandmother, inherited it in 1976.

Que Mongo.

Chapter 26
El Paso City, By the Rio Grande

You go through life working hard, studying hard, and traveling extensively just to make something of yourself or prove yourself at least. Then you get that degree; you pass that big exam; you make that big paycheck. There you go. You are an "all things" expert. As a Ph.D. in Psychology, you can explain the intricacies of the Social Security system. As an MD, you know how to invest your money wisely. As the head of a small law firm, you can explain the complicated sociology of the ever-changing place where you grew up. Except you can't. You are out of your element and, oops, your hubris is showing. You miss the biggest point on the biggest issue because you are, quite simply, blind. The case I was working on had an element that I completely ignored as important because, in my worldview, Odessa was white and black. Mexicans and Mexican-Americans were all around me, but other than Tex-Mex food, I paid little attention. Freddie died, and my focus was on her black husband, her part-time white lover, and his no-goodnik white partners--who just happened to be bringing into Odessa brown girls from Juarez, Mexico to serve as prostitutes!

Freddie would have been upset with this operation, yes, but what impact would it have on the Hispanic community in town? Would it bring in unsavory elements? Would it threaten Odessa's Hispanic girls? Would it bring more police to the south side? Would it cause a turf war among Odessa criminals? What was the Brown perspective?

Larraine Garza was going to explain all this to me, but first things first.

"Oh, boy, could you cover a kick-off. I loved those games and you were the first high school player I paid any attention to. Number 63 busts the wedge, grabs the back's jersey and spins him down to the ground. Whoo boy!"

"Oh, I do remember that play. You paid attention to me? How about that? You know, I rarely got to play other than on kick-offs?"

"I did not really notice that you didn't play because I was mostly there to watch my nephew, Ramon. We moved here from Ft. Stockton specifically to get him into Permian's district, so he could play. I left Odessa to get married to a Ft. Stockton guy and I was raising a family there and working on the newspaper. When my sister died, Ramon needed to live with us and he was a good football player. My husband and I decided to move to Odessa to take him in and learn my dad's business. I got into football. I watched all his games and the Panthers were my team."

"Yeah, he was really tough. What year did you come back here?"

"1975, boom times."

We sat in her office at the *Diario*. It was small and windowless, but it exuded authority with its leather chairs, pictures on the wall of Freddie Fender, Dallas Cowboy, Rafael Septien, Cezar Chavez, and Bill Clinton. The building from the outside looked like a regular print shop, like a place my dad would go to get brochures to post on telephone poles, but inside three people worked on stacking and packing many, many copies of a small newspaper. The *Diario* was not a fancy product. It was simply printed off on a small letter-press machine and it had tons of ads, very little artwork, and only one or two short informative articles. The most important section of the paper announced events around town that informed the Hispanic community about the rodeos, bingo games, school productions, graduations, weddings and obituaries in the community. The exploding influx of people coming to that part of town at the time would eventually create a whole new Odessa.

"Did you write anything about Freddie's murder back in '79?"

"No, her story was not fit to print, but she was important," she said.

"How so?"

"Well, you will have to get the details from others, but people were telling me several months before she died that those stupid Carleton boys were getting prostitutes from the barrio to go to parties for them on the other side. Every community has prostitutes, but the Odessa cops more or less left ours alone if they didn't disrupt polite, that is white, society. The main thing Slim Gabriel did as Sheriff to clean up Odessa in the 1950s was to move prostitution inside and off the streets. That was too much like the Wild West. But in 1979 it was the Wild 70s and the Carletons were reckless. We worried that those idiots would bring more cops here since they'd rather hassle the girls than target the greedy pimps who hired them."

"Yeah, I am learning how it works," I said.

"We don't like prostitution in the first place, but these guys paid the girls a little more and, well, the money

105

was tempting to the poor girls. Freddie helped stop that. Her friend, Rosa, worked for Freddie, but she refused to go to the parties."

"Rosa!" I thought.

Rosa got Freddie to come talk to the Hispanic Odessa girls about their personal safety and their health risks. She explained that problem one was those guys just didn't care if the girls were safe, if condoms were used, or if the cops would come our way."

"Yeah, Freddie took care of her people."

"Could be and that's good, but these were also tense times for us. You know anything about the Larry Ortega Lozano case?" she asked.

"Lozano?" I asked.

"He was a young man from Pecos who was not all right in the head. In 1978, here in Odessa, he got arrested for speeding and fought with the police. They put him in jail for assaulting a police officer. While awaiting trial, he got beat up and choked. He died. It was a wrongful death and even the US Justice Department got called in. Eventually the all-white investigation team ruled it an accident, saying he injured himself banging his head on the jail bars. Well, how did he get a crushed larynx from that? Good folks and hotheads in this community were very upset, still are, really, but then we also worried about police retaliation. It was a grave injustice and this community was about to explode at about the time the Carletons were being aggressive in getting girls. If cops learned about their efforts, they probably would have used any excuse to come in and bust some of our heads. This community was divided on how far to go on Lozano and whether the Carleton operation was going to draw the cops to us. Freddie defused it by reducing the numbers of our girls involved, but somehow in the end that just made things worse."

Larraine was a dignified woman. She had dark black hair streaked with gray. Her very practical black business suit was well served by a red scarf and expensive black pumps. And here she was talking about the prostitution business. But it was important, and Freddie brought a modicum of sanity to the situation. Unfortunately, it did not stop the Carletons.

Once the Carletons could not get Odessa Hispanic girls or even West Texas girls, they decided to go get some from Juarez, Mexico. West Texas boys from hundreds of miles away had always gone there and now these guys wanted the girls to come to Odessa. There were all kinds of bad in that. Since they offered more money than the pimps did in Mexico, some girls found their way over. The bad hombres in Juarez were furious. Odessa cops were unaware. Freddie and her business were threatened. The Carletons thought they were getting away with it, but everyone who knew about it on the south side was determined to shut it down before we had open warfare on the streets. The Carletons were essentially stealing from the Mexican gangs. It was what you'd call Bad Mojo.

Of course, Freddie could not stop this alone. She had to bring muscle to bear and it had to be sudden and complete. She recruited a small army of black toughs under Willie Gumble and Hispanic toughs through contacts Rosa helped her find. The plan was to swoop in on the place where the Carletons brought the girls to rest and dress before the party they had arranged after hours at the Golden Hotel downtown. That place?

The decrepit barn on Old Crane Highway.

Chapter 27
The Plot Thickens

Every step forward in the investigation also raised big questions. How did the Hispanic community learn that the Carletons would turn to trying to get girls from Juarez? How did Freddie know how to organize a raid on the barn? She was no criminal or military mastermind. The answer to both questions was Willie Gumble. How I found out about that came unexpectedly and from an unlikely source, Freddie's ex, Cleon, with whom I visited one more time to probe his story about his whereabouts on the night Freddie died.

This time we did not meet at the church. I wanted no one to see me talking to him, so I called on JayJay for help. She got in touch with Cleon and made arrangements to pick him up at night and bring him to my Lee Street office. Downtown Odessa was virtually empty on Saturday nights since the Scott movie theater had shuttered its doors in '87 and the Ector Theater two blocks south of it on Golder Street had not yet reopened for special events. I walked to my office, JayJay left Cleon off in the driveway, and we closed the blinds in my office. That way we hoped no one could see us talking.

I came to the front door as soon as Cleon approached. He was wearing overalls, a blue work shirt, tattered back shoes and white socks. He looked every bit the maintenance man he was, but he also looked worried. After grabbing a Diet Coke for me and a glass of orange juice for Cleon, we settled in to talk. Thank goodness M.A. had put in a small couch in my office. Cleon sat there, and I pulled my chair from behind the desk over closer to the couch. I wanted Cleon to feel more comfortable.

I started with general chit-chat about his health and the weather, but he interrupted:

"Mr. Covey, I appreciate the O.J. but Miss Bonnie say you need to talk and I 'ma pretty sure it's not about tornado season."

"Well, you're right about that, so I'll just get to the nitty-gritty."

"All right then."

"I have one person who says you did leave Fat's in your car the night Freddie died."

"Oh, shit...excuse me, Mr. Covey."

"Not to worry, Cleon. What is it you haven't told me?"

"Well, the truth is what I told you, but for the sake of livin' let's jes go back to the official story. I drove my drunk-ass over to the barn and kilt the woman I still loved and my onliest source of money at the time."

"Who had you beat up down in Huntsville?"

"Oh, Lord, you know too much now. I ain't sayin'!" Cleon said.

"But you know?"

"I know."

"Let's take it another direction. You have any idea why Freddie was at the barn the night she died?"

"She got took there I suspect," he said.

"Yeah? Was something going on there?"

"Not that night far as I know but two-three nights before, you bet."

It took an hour and a lot of reassurances to convince Cleon to tell me at least part of what he knew. Willie had promised to break him in half if he ever let go of secrets he had carried a long way for a long time. I think he told me to relieve himself of a burden and to clear his conscience late in life.

Someone, and he would not say his name (but I knew it was Willie), drove to and from El Paso a lot. That person on occasion visited the whore houses in Juarez. One night, while drinking and watching a stage show at the Swank Club, that person saw two Odessa white men talking to his favorite girl. Later she told that person that the men wanted her to recruit other girls to come to Odessa just every once in a while. That person later told Miss Freddie about this threat to her business. Miss Freddie confided this to Cleon. He wished that he had never known about it.

Now I knew about it and at the end of the night, I knew even more than that but, once again, I had more questions. About one thing I felt certain. Cleon, the reformed man, was still not telling me the whole truth and now both of us had better tread carefully.

The other thing I knew, and the secret I promised never to reveal to anyone, was that Willie's favorite girl in Juarez, the one who told him about the Carletons, was no girl. She was a he who performed in drag. And with tears in his eyes Cleon "confessed" to me that he, too, back then, you know, also liked to dress like a woman on occasion, and sometimes, though he didn't like it, run his mouth on a big man. Freddie loved him anyway and no one else could ever know this "horrible secret about his ways back then."

111

Chapter 28
March 1979

The long trip from El Paso was not well planned. The connection with the ten girls at 8:30 AM at a dingy motel on the outskirts of El Paso went pretty well, but the Carletons were shocked when the girls, for the most part, spoke little English. No one in the five Texans' cars knew any Spanish beyond "Como esta usted?" Improvised sign language would have to do. The girls had overnight bags with a change of clothes and personal necessities. The suitcases were fairly big and all old. The car trunks had not been emptied for anticipated luggage and it took a long while to squeeze everything in. The boys had planned on a six-hour trip, but even by taking Interstate 10 to El Paso the day before, it had taken six-and-a-half hours just from city limit to city limit and no one planned the effect of bathroom stops or food breaks on the return.

Going back by the old U.S. Highway 80 and thus avoiding the Interstate was their clever idea of stealth, but that route was longer, the fast food chains were scarcer, and the tempers flared even more frequently, especially between brothers Delbert, Jr. and Aaron. By the end of the eleven-hour journey Wild Bill was disgusted with the brothers and the two other barely-older-than-teenage drivers were exhausted. In truth all were worn out, especially the girls, and by the 8:00 PM arrival in Odessa there was almost no time to rest before changing for the 11:00 PM party. They had to make an unscheduled stop at a motel, send the young drivers home, let the girls fix up and use the facilities, before taking two trips to shuttle the girls to the barn where they had stored skimpy outfits.

Scouting their arrival at the barn, on the other hand, was easy. Willie did not know the party day for sure, but he assumed a weekend night, so every Friday and Saturday for a month to six weeks before, he drove by the barn an hour or so after the sun went down. Once or twice he set out just as the sun disappeared in the distant west as its deep yellow glow mixed with the low-hanging dark clouds to produce one of the eeriest and most beautiful sights a human could ever witness. Viet Nam had nothing like this. Okinawa had nothing to compare. He had never been there, but surely New York City blocked the sky and hid its mysteries. Like all West Texans, Willie felt that his access to a Texas sky provided a freedom and safe harbor that few other places afforded, but he had never been other places to know for sure. But he had been to Viet Nam and when the Carleton brothers showed up, they would not present the same challenge as the Viet Cong. Both then and now, the element of surprise would work in his favor-when it ever was to happen.

March 19, 1979 was to be the night. Willie cruised by the barn twice, at 8:00 PM and again at 9:30 PM. The second time the two cars were obvious, and one was the Big Red. One car was literally at the barn door and one was parked as close to the barn it could get by the dirt road leading from the highway. Because Willie had broken into the place quite easily a few weeks before, he knew how the interior was laid out. Using an over-sized lantern, he had inspected the place thoroughly. The inside was not exactly clean, but there was no horse manure and no obvious signs

113

of rats. Someone had been cleaning up the place because there was fresh hay in the stalls and there were tables of various sizes placed here and there. As a temporary way station. it might work, but surely no one was supposed to sleep in this place. Willie did a couple of things before he left. The back door was secured by a wooden arm slid into two metal handles. It took a while to remove the screws from the handles and replace them with thinner screws that would not hold if the door was slammed from the outside, but Willie did it. The board inside the handles would look secure, but it was not. The other item for Willie was to place the lantern under a bucket along the outside barn wall just to have a backup, if necessary, come the big night. You can never be too careful.

Willie saw the cars and set the plan in action. He drove to a nearby 7-11. One call to Rosa and one call to Cleon led to a series of calls to others both black and Hispanic. It may have been one of the most successful collaborations ever between the two communities. Thirty minutes later, by plan, a half-dozen cars met in an empty lot just beyond the I-20 underpass close to Texas Road 385, what Odessans call the Old Crane Highway. Every person there had a rifle or a handgun. Willie was in charge. but Jose Blanco barked Willie's orders in Spanish. They were united in stopping the Carletons, helping Freddie, and protecting south side's communities. Five minutes later, they took off for the barn.

Upon arriving, Willie took note that the Carleton cars were still there and that there was light emanating from the inside. He had worried slightly about the timing, but the men and girls were still there and, of course, they had posted no sentry. Willie rightly figured the brothers had used connections to avoid military service and thus military training. Muted voices came from the inside that Willie took for loud whispering. It reminded him of small children who shut their eyes and thought they could not be seen.

The whole thing took three minutes. After dividing and deploying their troops front and back, Willie, assuming rearguard command, waited at the back door with 7 men. Jose, standing in front with another 6 men, waited 2 minutes before banging loudly on the door and yelling: "Police, open up!"

Willie heard the panic inside and then gave the sign to three guys to charge the backdoors, hit them like they would block a linebacker, and bust it open. Willie and the others then charged in behind into the barn brandishing their weapons. The girls had run into the stalls, Aaron stood motionless, Bill got knocked down by the door because he was the only one to think of running away from the knocking, and Delbert stood in the middle holding an unloaded shotgun. Willie's men quickly surrounded and disarmed them. Jose and his men grabbed the women and took them to the cars. Delbert, Jr. started to speak, "You sons a-bitches..."

Willie stopped him with "Shut the fuck up, Cracker, or I'll drop you where you stand!"

Delbert nodded.

Willie continued: "These girls come with us. Do not follow or you're dead. Do not try this again or we will give your names to the thugs in Juarez and we will be sure to take you to them if they want us to. Let the Odessa cops know and off you go to Juarez."

He started to leave and then said, "Hope Y'all have a good rest of the night."

That part of the operation over, Willie allowed himself to smile and laugh at the idiots. He did not, however, anticipate what he'd hear when the team reconnoitered back at the empty lot. Jose got right to the point.

"Willie, man, we got a problemo."

"What's up, Jose?"

"Man, them girls don't wanna go back? They wanna stay in the U.S. They had to sneak out. They don't wanna sneak back in."

"Damn, how bout they families, they bosses?" Willie asked.

"They are 'fraid of the bosses and don't say nothing about families," Jose said.

Willie now faced a real dilemma, but it got worse. After letting the girls go with Jose to put them in the prearranged homes where they would hide for the night, he went to his apartment to think. His message machine blinked like crazy. It turned out that Larraine Garza, the *Diario* owner, had been trying to reach him all day. Hector Villarilla, she informed him, owner of the "Swank Club" in Juarez had called her to send a message. He had figured out that the two white men talking to China (pronounced Cheena) in the club were from Odessa and Willie, he knew, was from Odessa. Hector also knew Larraine was in Odessa. She would get his message: If Willie knew where the girls were or if by chance he had them, he'd better get them back to Juarez pronto or China would lose part of her anatomy very important to Willie.

116

No matter what Willie did or did not know Hector was holding him accountable.

He had 48 hours to make it happen.

Chapter 29
The Plan

A lot of things happen below the white radar in Odessa, Texas. The poor whites and all the black and brown folks near or across the tracks have full lives that simply go unnoticed. It's only in part because of the trailers, small houses, or ratty apartments these citizens occupy. Yes, they are physically removed from the old established west side houses or the new McMansions already showing up east of John Ben Shepard Blvd. and the new University of the Permian Basin (UTPB), but that's not the whole thing. Racism, privileged white lack of interest, and persons of color's desire to live normal lives and be left the hell alone meant there was minimal interaction between the communities. And that interaction was further limited by routine and unspoken rules. Folks like JayJay and the owners of Tex-Mex restaurants knew those rules and did what they could to be part of the commercial life of Odessa while making few waves. But they knew the rules. Folks like Willie and Jose also knew the rules, but the rage they felt inside pretty much kept them on the south side as much as possible. And the south side was a reality that very few white Odessans even imagined or cared to know. In fact, they feared it.

In March 1979, parts of the south side were alarmed at the prospect of attracting Mexican thugs to Odessa or conversely returning girls to Juarez to what increasingly looked like indentured servitude in the Mexican prostitution world. Of course, there were voices arguing that the girls should be allowed to stay in the U.S and asserting that the gang threats were not credible. Two of the latter were friends of Larraine Garza whom she asked to represent her. Others more street-wise, like Willie, Cleon, and Jose, knew that in prisons in South Texas, Mexican gangs already had a presence and someday, but not this day, they hoped, they might just show up in Odessa. They also worried that despite their warnings to the Carletons, perhaps those idiots would somehow involve the Odessa police who would, most likely, believe whatever lies those white men told as opposed to the truth.

Freddie ran the meeting in the backroom at Fatman's. She let every voice be heard. It was in mid-afternoon and there were no customers. "Respectable" members of the black and brown communities were not there, but everyone in the room knew that all people on the south side could be affected by the results of the meeting. Ultimately the group decided they had to consider the greater good in rendering a decision. Freddie Mae's argument eventually won the day:

"We have to take them girls back, but we got to explain that we didn't take them in the first place. We got to convince Hector that we ain't no way connected to that Carleton bunch."

Jose said, "I will go over to his club alone and unarmed to explain it."

Willie piped in. "No way, man, they would just take you hostage and probably kill you if they don't get all the girls back."

Freddie said, "We got to take every one of them girls back, but we can't take them to Mexico. Take

119

'em to El Paso, drop them at an agreed upon place, and then say adios. They got phones in Mexico, right?"

She did not wait for a response.

"Tell Miss Larraine to call this fella Hector to give us a place in or around El Paso and we will get them there. We ain't fuckin' with Border Patrol and he knows how to get folks in and out of Mexico."

"What do we tell the girls?" Willie asked.

"Part of the truth," said Freddie, "the part about taking them to El Paso."

Jose chimed in, "It's tough but I think it's right. But it's tough."

"Yeah," said Freddie, "it's tough. But let's get it goin'. Sooner it's over, the better."

Secretly, Willie felt personal relief over the decision, but he was unsure if he could ever go back to the Swank Club to see China. The next day he, Jose, and two other drivers gathered up the girls in vans and headed for El Paso.

The trouble was not over.

Chapter 30
March 21, 1979

Freddie hated to send the girls back. She hated to be in the prostitution business in the first place, but she hated being poor more. Her own mother turned to prostitution after becoming a single mom at 16. The bastard she was with both abused her and then skipped town when she got pregnant. Freddie, their child, grew up on the margins of a marginal town very close to the swamp in Oberlin, Louisiana, but she also grew up to be a resourceful girl. She got little education and dropped out completely when her friend Gro said he and his brothers were heading to Odessa, Texas where an oil boom was creating all kinds of jobs, even some for black folks. At first Freddie did not catch on at the Car Wash where Gro worked so she temporarily turned to hooking to make ends meet. She had common sense and good instincts, so she made it OK. But, she said, "There are some crazy white men in Odessa, Texas!" Frank Jencks was less crazy than most and finally he gave her a job. Freddie did what she had to do. Jesus said to care for the sick and the poor. Freddie was poor and sometimes she was sick. She would take care of herself first.

As she got older, Freddie saw a pattern for poor girls with single moms. More and more she saw herself as part of this pattern and more and more she saw helping those girls as also helping herself. It became a purpose in life. But she would have none of the do-gooders who claimed to want to help. From the black Baptist preacher in Oberlin who tried to feel her body to the welfare folks in Odessa who often treated single moms with either hostility or cold indifference, she saw them as outsiders who did not realize that folks just want to make it on their own. She, just like any cowboy or any oil man, wanted respect. It's a simple instinct and a hard goal to accomplish. Especially for a poor black girl from Louisiana living in West, By God, Texas. But she knew what all West Texans knew: To get respect, you gots to earn it. She would never act the fool.

The Juarez girls were like her and she knew it, but there was nothing she could do about it. Too many things could go wrong in Odessa and in Juarez if she tried to set them free. What a funny concept, she thought. Freddie Mae Johnson setting anyone free! No, they had made the right decision. Best to send those girls back. Best to protect her own girls. Best to keep south Odessa safe. Best to keep the wolves from the door. At that very second, just past midnight on March 22, 1979, someone knocked on her door. The long day and the long night were not over. There was no way not to open the door, but as she slipped on a light blue duster, she did not know what was ahead. She just knew she had to face it.

Bill O'Toole stood on her porch, looking this way and that, waiting for Freddie to answer his knock. There were no car lights and no street lights to illuminate his presence.

Chapter 31
Who Do You Trust?

Freddie had to answer the door that fateful night in 1979. She feared that Bill O'Toole knew she had been involved with the girls' rescue and she worried he would cause trouble if she tried to lock him out. But maybe not; maybe he was unaware. Whatever, she thought, "I can handle this." She knew that his weakness, shared by many a man, was what she was willing to do for him sexually. Call it manipulation or call it what you wish, it usually worked. Either he knew her role in the rescue or he didn't, but Freddie's way out would be the same no matter what.

Before the knock, she had thought the night was over. She had gone to Fatman's earlier on a tip from Willie that Cleon did not show up to help take the Mexican girls back to El Paso. She went to Fat's to assure herself that Cleon had once again succumbed to drink as he usually did when he was wracked by guilt and shame. When she found him, he was already on his way to being drunk, but he was all right. No cops or bad white men had picked off the team's weakest link. She refused him money for hooch, but he was all right. Now hours later, this. She would do what she had to do. She did not put on day clothes.

Bill was alone, and his tone was soothing.

"Come on baby, come talk to me."

Freddie said, "Nah, not here. Not your place. Not tonight."

"Let's go for a ride. It's a nice night. Look at them stars."

She dared not ask about the Carleton boys. Maybe it was a booty call. She hoped it was a booty call. Maybe he did not know she was involved.

He knew. Or at least he assumed. More than once he had seen her talk to Willie Gumble when he showed up at the car wash.

Chapter 32
It's Complicated: Back to the 90s

JayJay had it right: "To figure out what happened in 1979, to solve the mystery of who killed Freddie and why, we have to locate the Carleton brothers and Wild Bill O'Toole," JayJay said. "We have gone as far as we can with the folks on the south side. We need more information. We have to sort out the respective roles of Cleon Johnson, Willie Gumble, Bill O'Toole and both Aaron and Delbert Carleton in the matter of her death. Any one of them seemed to have motive and opportunity at the time."

To which I added: "I agree. And I am sure that all three of the white guys left Odessa at one time or another. M.A. has searched the computer and found likely suspects named Aaron A. Carleton in McKinney, Texas and Delbert P. Carleton in nearby Frisco, Texas. She has not found Wild Bill, but she wants me to talk to Beth again instead of her—pretty sensitive territory there."

"I think I know someone else we can approach," JayJay said.

"Oh, yeah, who?"

"There's another guy who sometimes comes in for service for his Toyota Lexus, a Mr. Baker. He has a military bearing and is just about the nicest person you ever met. His name is Frederick Baker, but a couple of days ago, Mr. Tiner, you know our GM, called him something else."

"Which was?" I asked.

"Junior."

"Junior Baker? The detective who investigated Freddie's murder?"

Dan Gladstone had found Freddie's dead body for the Odessa Police Department, but Detective Junior Baker conducted the investigation.

"I'm not certain but could be. Just in case I copied down his address and phone number. Don't tell on me," JayJay added.

I had thought to talk to Dan Gladstone, but I had been reluctant to look for Baker. I made assumptions about his probable racist attitudes and likely motivations to protect police misconduct that just warned me off, especially in light of the message on my car at Ratliff Stadium. What if there had been a police conspiracy back in '79? After talking with JayJay a bit, I re-examined my prejudices. JayJay had in fact known Junior Baker for years. He was nice to everyone and he was always polite, even gentle. He once brought JayJay a small batch of flowers when he heard that her mama had died, and it was pure kindness with no sexual overtones, unlike some of the other gestures by other "nice" men. And she did not tell him that she had not shed a tear on her mother's death. If this guy was a cop of any kind, he sure did not seem like one. He also seemed not to be working as he was clearly well into his 70s. We both wondered how he could afford a Lexus.

"Junior" Baker would be my next person to contact. JayJay decided that she, not I, would talk to Beth about her dad, Wild Bill. She didn't know for sure, but if there was anything like abuse in Beth's relationship with Bill, maybe another woman could ease the discussion.

Of course, I needed J's help with Baker as well. Would he be irritated by a phone call out of the blue? Would JayJay's call be an abuse of her position at Sewell's? How would I start the conversation? Oh, I don't know, will the sky fall on Tuesday? JayJay shut down my worried speculation with:

"Why don't I just ask him to meet you for coffee when he picks up his car next week?" she asked.

"Hmm, that might work."

She did, and he said yes, but he added, "What's this about?"

She asked him to confirm that he had been a detective, which he did. So, she said it was about an old case.

"Is it Lozano?"

"No, Freddie Johnson," she said.

"How about that? That is the other case that convinced me to resign."

It turns out that Junior Baker left the Odessa Police Department to become the Department of Justice's chief investigator in West Texas. From the military police in Germany to Odessa Detective to DOJ, Baker had three pensions, a frugal nature, and a three-decade marriage to a nice lady from Queens, New York, who happened to be Jewish."

Golly.

We did not meet downtown at the Cafe. Better to go out to the Holiday Inn Express restaurant just outside the loop on East 8th St.

"Mr. Baker, thank you for meeting me. I hate to dredge up painful memories."

127

"Pleasure is mine, Mr. Jencks. I am intrigued by what you think you can do about this case. I agree it has not been solved."

"Frankly, that seems odd. You got credit for solving the case in the first place," I said.

"Yes and no. I thought her husband the likely culprit, but other things needed clearing up,"

"The knife?" I wondered.

"The knife, the blood found close to the barn, the recent vehicular activity. Lots."

"Let me guess. Higher ups already had their scapegoat," I said.

"In part and, in part, the Lozano case weighed heavily on everyone's mind. There were political considerations, sure. Then there's the fact that her husband lied."

"About what?" I asked.

"He said he never left that BBQ place, but he did. In fact, we know he was with another man and that he engaged in a sexual act not four blocks away from where we found Freddie. That never came out in his trial in agreement with his lawyer. Keeping that secret seemed to be a bigger deal than almost anything else and we bargained down to a manslaughter charge. It was as good as a confession."

"How did you find out?" I wondered.

"We had witnesses see him leave Fatman's. We confronted Cleon and he told us the truth. We think that guy he had sex with took him back to the BBQ place and his car. We signed a document never to reveal his secret to the public and you are the first person I have ever told. The fact

128

was that he still had time both to kill her and to get back to the restaurant, but I thought it improbable."

"So?"

"So, the incredible hostility on the south side toward the police and a likely suspect made it an easy choice. I objected to closing the case and I also objected to the argument that we needed a quick fix due to football recruiting considerations. I mean, a life was at stake. I was helpless on both counts, but I did see why the brass went the way they did."

He continued. "The unaddressed issues for me remained, but the DA asked if I thought we had enough to prosecute. In all honesty I did, but it all gnawed on me."

"Did you know of a white-run prostitution ring and a plan to bring in Mexican women?"

"Not at the time, but later we had a massage parlor scandal later on and a lot of 'prominent' citizens were caught up in it. During that, we learned that operation was in part inspired by some nonsense at the Legion Hall. Shameful stuff actually."

"Did you have any ideas about who ran the Legion Hall shenanigans?" I asked.

"Rumors only about the idiot Carleton brothers. They left town soon after Freddie died, and they owned the property next to where she died. I wanted to go after them, but the argument was that we had our man in Huntsville. When DOJ came calling, I was more than happy to get to serve law enforcement another way."

"Did you encounter racism in the Odessa PD?" I asked.

"We are in America, aren't we?"

129

Then he added. "Well, just as we only prosecute acts, not the worms that squirm around some brains, we also have to live with the biases that we all have."

"I am going after the Carletons and maybe Bill O'Toole. Want to help?"

"I am not a vigilante and I ask you not to be one either. But, if you do, my money is on the really stupid one, Aaron," Baker said.

Chapter 33
Talkin' 'Bout My Situation

"We never talk about race."

JayJay sat up in the bed and looked at me.

"Oh God, you aren't gonna ask me how it feels to be black, are you? Or if I wish I were white?"

"No, but something Baker said to me has been rattling around my brain," I said.

"Hmm, did he say you think too much?"

"No, I believe he may think I don't know enough about the real world to be a detective. He said we all have biases and we just have to work around them. Acts, not beliefs, are what matter."

"Sure, that's right," she replied.

"I really thought I didn't have that many prejudices. I mean other than knowing that all the people over in Midland are rich snobs and all their kids are spoiled."

"I have mine, for sure. I have a terrible attitude toward fat white women. And, no, I don't feel the same about black women," she said.

"Baker seems to think we just have to live with the fact of bias, especially the bias of others. But this new thing called political correctness. I am not sure what I think about it. It can't change the way folks really think, but maybe it can affect behavior or ease the sting of language. Ya suppose?" I wondered.

"Shit, Liberal Boy, I don't know. I doubt it and I know it will be hard for me to go there."

"Yeah, you are too salty for that, but you'd never say something tacky to Erica or Alberto, right?"

"Of course not, but since you are getting all personal now, let's talk about sex," she said.

"Sex? What about sex? We have great sex!"

"Yes, we do," she said, "but I also know your past alley cat life and I know what Freddie told me about men. They are capable of living two lives and they have itches they have to scratch. They fantasize about black women, but over time they start thinking about other women, too. Variety and the spice of life, you know. I mean, you dated me back in high school because you got struck by Jungle Fever. Come the day, will I stop turning you on? We all have worries, you know!" she said.

"Oh, shit, JayJay! This is not Jungle Fever. You know, I also worry if I am man enough for you, but…but damn, you are asking about lust and not love. I will tell you as a man, …fuck, you are still the hottest girl I ever met."

"OK then, and if that changes, you have to tell me. You have to! We have to be totally open about this!"

"Yes, Mam, yes. That is also very hot. Anything else you want to know?" I asked.

"No, but I know that it is motherfucking 1:00 AM and I have to be at work at 7:00 AM or da man gonna fire my black ass. So, go to sleep, Cracker. I'll leave your white bread and milk on the kitchen cabinet in da mornin'. Now help me relax so's I can sleep."

"Thanks, JayJay, nice talk."

I did sleep well that night. I felt that JayJay and I were even closer, and I felt that the new information from Junior Baker and Larraine Garza moved us nearer to the parties responsible for Freddie's death. I was determined to see things through to the end. Whoever committed the act of killing Freddie, whoever let his greed, prejudice, or hatred run wild, had to be held accountable. If no one else on earth cared who killed her, JayJay and I did. We were one in the search for justice.

Chapter 34
Truth and Consequences

The inescapable fact was that the white guys had run. Willie's operation had busted their prostitution ring. Freddie had played a big role in organizing that bust. One black guy had not run because he had already gone to jail for the crime and his lying might or might not relate to the murder. It seemed more and more likely that his lying was simply the biggest, darkest, most lonely closet that any man could ever endure. The other guy, the man with the fighter's body and a quick temper, could kill but really seemed unlikely to have done so. Our leading candidates then were white, the last guy we knew she was with (Bill) but also the stupid one (Aaron), and the greedy one (Delbert). We had to narrow down the likeliest candidate and find out who did it.

Here's what we eventually came to realize. Once you have done something, it's impossible to act as if it didn't happen. As much as the Carletons didn't want anyone to die, Freddie did. As much as Delbert wanted to be rich, he couldn't be. As much as Wild Bill wanted things to be normal, that could not happen. While the Odessa Police never came looking to talk to any of them, they had problems galore. Life would never be the same. They had to run.

The first problem for the "brains of the operation" was the money. Half of it was gone. Delbert returned the other half to the Golden Hotel manager to give back to the men .50 cents on the dollar. That guy offered to cover the other $5 K if Delbert would repay him another $10 K. If not, the manager knew some folks in Dallas who were expert debt collectors. Delbert sold "the Red," drew down his savings, and borrowed from another friend to get $10 K. In 1979 it was a serious financial setback.

One thing Delbert did not do. He did not ask his brother for a dime and he did not discuss the arrangements he had struck. Delbert and Aaron in fact never spoke again. Their admittedly half-baked trafficking plan did attract unwanted attention and outsider intervention. It was doomed from the start. Delbert blamed Aaron for everything that went wrong at the barn, but, of course, that was unfair. But Aaron always got in trouble and he always brought Delbert down with him. Delbert knew that if the cops ever showed up at his door, he'd tell them all and do whatever time he had coming. Delbert left Odessa in late 1979, ended up in Florida selling timeshare condos for a few years, and finally settled in the Dallas area where he got into selling over-priced homes in the Plano/Frisco area. He occasionally saw some Odessa people out there but the weight he put on and the beard he grew kept him unrecognizable. He didn't feel the need to change his name, but he began using his middle name at all times. Now folks called him Parker.

Bill was disturbed by the turn of events. He had really liked Freddie. Too bad she died the way she did. He hated that his chance for steady money had evaporated. He liked to pose as a hotshot and imply that he had been important in Boston and to Frank Jencks. Had he really been a player in Boston or had he been more gofer than boss? He did not run a prostitution ring. He collected for it and did other "odd jobs," some of which involved heavy lifting. When some money went missing, he ran to Odessa to escape the bad guys, not the cops. Frank Jencks hired him for part-time weekend work at the car wash simply to have a white face collecting the money. Gro always ran the place. Bill received minimum wage for his labors.

Bill's wife divorced him because he had no money and no prospects most of all. She started working at, then managing, a Mode O'Day shop in downtown Odessa and she and Beth made it on their own. Beth never heard a good word about Bill, but he had never hurt her, and he never abused her. Bill was a loser always looking for a score, but he never found one and Freddie's death ended his search. He left Odessa because of his role in Freddie's death and because he feared a Carleton decision to bump him off. He decided to go to a little town he saw on the map called Deming, New Mexico. No one would find him there. Maybe he'd like other things to do.

But who killed Freddie?

Chapter 35
Daddy Issues

To find who killed Freddie, JayJay and I literally had to track down the three principal actors. We decided to start with the person for whom we had the closest tie at hand: Wild Bill O'Toole whose daughter, Beth, was one easy phone call away in Odessa.

Elizabeth O'Toole actually missed her daddy. The older she got, the more she saw that her mom had flaws as much as her dad did. Her mom was not really warm and fuzzy, and she had no capacity to find humor in anything. Her dad was loud, boastful, and always quick with a story. Just like Beth.

Her mom at least did not push her towards boys, Beth always bragged. The truth was that lady hated men and the small version of people who would become men. Beth was OK with men. She was just not that sexually attracted to them and, yes, she took a number of test drives.

Beth always said she hated Bill and did not wish ever to see him again, but his leaving without saying good-bye hurt a little more each year. She told JayJay these things after the conversation "got real" when JayJay told her own daddy stories.

"So, Beth, do you have any idea at all where he is now?"

"All my mom said was that he was going farther west. I kinda dreamed that meant California, but I didn't know."

There are a couple of things I have never told anyone, not even M.A."

"Yeah?" letting Beth go on.

"Well, after Bill left, maybe two days later, I opened my mom's desk and there was $200 and a piece of paper that said, 'For Beth.' To me, it was his goodbye, but I never got a penny of it."

"And the other?"

"I don't know how much longer after that I saw my mom tear up a postcard. I snuck in later and saw that it had a New Mexico postmark. In my mind, I figured it was from my daddy and he was not too far away, but like I say, I don't know."

Chapter 36
Tony Hillerman Land

Growing up I always had a bad attitude about New Mexico. Based on nothing more than one drive through to go to the Grand Canyon with Jack and his parents when we were in Junior High, I always thought of New Mexico as West Texas without oil. I even assumed that the Carlsbad Caverns were in Texas and not in New Mexico. I think my bad attitude derived from my dad's obsession with going to Ruidoso, N.M. or more specifically Ruidoso Downs, where he drank, bet on the horses, and generally cavorted with other semi-rich Texans. Over time, I heard of the artist colony in and around Santé Fe and in the Army, I had occasion to learn the history of the development of the atomic bomb and the national lab at Sandia. Naturally somewhere in there, I heard about Area 51 and the silly speculations about alien invasion in Roswell. Of course, I knew little about the Native American history or the Spanish presence in the 15th and 16th centuries. As a kid, I just knew that they may have had a good basketball team in Hobbs, but the worst football or baseball team in West Texas, we were told, could beat the best such teams in New Mexico. As JayJay and I drove into New Mexico on I-10, at least I now had sense enough to know that while my eyes were seeing West Texas without oil, my brain knew that there much more to the story. OK, I said to myself, I have to read Tony Hillerman and his stories about Navajo detectives.

JayJay was excited to go through the state. When she was at Ector High and a cheerleader, she went to a cheerleader camp in Las Cruces, NW, and had a great time. Everyone was so nice there and the squads were not universally white and snooty. What I knew about Las Cruces is that you turn left there to get to Deming. We were on our way in hopes of finding Wild Bill O'Toole. By our calculations, he was now 71 or 72. His address was on East Maple just south of the highway. We had not attempted to write or call, and we were not even certain that this was "our" William O'Toole. We took off one weekend in spring 1995 anyway in part to just get out of town and in part to continue our investigation. Beth's comments had modified our views somewhat. Maybe he was not a total monster or big-time gangster. My memories of him were slight. He showed up and worked some weekends at the car wash and he was forever laughing with and nudging the male customers, but I was not quite sure what to make of him.

From what JayJay had been able to determine, Bill had helped the idiot Carletons throw a wild party at the Legion Hall, had no doubt helped them try to bring girls in from Mexico, had a relationship with Freddie and probably knew something about her death. Well, he might even have killed her, for all we knew. Talking to him might prove a little difficult. We really had no plan other than to "bump" into him some way and let me take the lead based on our former car wash affiliation. JayJay might later weigh in about his daughter. But first, we had to find him.

We pulled into Deming at 9:07 PM. It had been over seven hours after leaving Odessa. We checked into a La Quinta Inn before we hit the streets (make that street) of

140

Deming. We had eaten at a Whataburger just outside of El Paso, so we did not need food. We did want to see what we could see in Deming, however, so we took a short spin. East Maple Street was easy to find but 312 was all dark. He had either retired early or he was out. We hoped that he was taking in the Deming party scene and not in fact out of town. Even in the dark the street and the town were scruffy and dusty. We decided to go north of the Interstate to explore. Not five minutes later we encountered "the Silver Bucket Saloon" just beyond I-10. It looked like a thriving operation, so we decided to drop in for a beer. I felt at home immediately. Johnny Cash was on the jukebox singing about "Sunday Morning Coming Down" and most people in there, white and shades of brown, wore cowboy hats and boots.

At first, I did not notice him. Wild Bill was sitting in a booth far to the right facing towards us as we walked in the door. The bar was to our left and there were two booths before Bill's to our right, then the wall, and five more booths straight across from the bar to Bill's right. At the far end to the left of the bar were a jukebox and an empty pool table. The bathrooms were down a hallway in the left corner. To sit down JayJay and I either had to sit at the bar or take the one unoccupied booth next to Bill and several patrons who sat nursing beers as Bill talked. JayJay did not hesitate to walk right to the booth next to Bill's.

He was holding court, Bill being Bill. Laughter mixed with reverential stares from adoring patrons and friends. As JayJay walked to the booth, Bill said:

"That Whitey was a tough nut, but he wouldn't dirty his hands on no nig…"

141

He looked up and saw a black face first and then he realized it was JayJay's face. His eyes darted to mine and his smile evaporated into the desert dust. He almost immediately picked up a coffee that he alone was drinking. He swallowed the last bit, excused himself from the group, and walked back toward the restrooms.

"I think he may be going out the back door," I said.

"Let's see," JayJay responded. "We are not going to follow him. We know where he lives."

The folks in the booth were quite aware that Bill had bolted because we came in. You could see them wondering if we were maybe from a Boston gang coming to whack Wild Bill, but they were unsure enough not to react. Finally, a lady said:

"Howdy, where Y'all from? Not from around here, I know."

"Odessa, I offered."

"Texas, eh, why does ever-body have to be from Texas?"

"Yeah, there are a lot of us, but we are the quiet ones, I said."

"Good deal then. Say, do you know Uncle William? He seemed to know you."

"Yes, he and my dad used to wash cars together."

"Oh, I see," she said.

Suddenly Bill was standing there.

"Bonnie Jay, my goodness you have grown up. I have thought of you often over the years. Are you good?"

"Hello, Mr. Bill, I am fine. Do you remember Covey Jencks here?"

I extended my hand, but he didn't take it. He pursed his lips and shook his head no.

"Son, you and your daddy are not welcome in my life. I am sure he is dead, and I don't mean to disrespect the dead, but he was a sorry son-of-a-bitch who still owes me $3,000 and you were nothing but disrespectful to me every time I ever saw you."

JayJay jumped in.

"Bill, this is my man and his daddy is still alive. We came a long way to talk to you about Freddie Mae. I promise Covey is not at all like his daddy and, for a lawyer, he is good people."

She smiled and Bill almost smiled.

"Freddie, huh? I guess I figured that. Well, not here and my place ain't suitable either. You folks have a motel room?"

I nodded yes. Bill turned to his admirers.

"Well, story time is over tonight folks. Come back to tomorrow and I will tell you all about the great Carl Yastrzemski in 1967 against the low-life Yankees."

He looked at JayJay. "I am often the entertainment here. I used to be the bartender, but now I get a free dinner and all the coffee I want just to tell my lies and stories. Best time of my life, but I guess it had to end sometime."

Chapter 37
Story Time

Getting Wild Bill to talk was not the problem. Getting him to stop was.

My concern was discerning how much of it was true. O'Toole was an Irishman with the gift of gab and the cliché about kissing the blarney stone applied to him. We stayed up almost all night. Bill took the one comfortable chair and JayJay and I sat on the bed propped up by pillows. Contrary to our plan, JayJay took the lead. We had to get past that little matter that he seemed to hate my guts. Mine was guilt by association with my daddy and my rather serious case of teenage hostility in 1977-78. Since I was hostile to Frank Jencks, I evidently extended it to Frank's friend, Bill O'Toole. I have to admit that seemed likely to me. The truth was that Bill, if anything, had a lower regard for Frank than I did, but he hung around to protect his investment.

To make a long story a little bit short, Frank and Bill met in Dallas in 1973 at a strip club called "The Peekers." Bill, just down from Boston, was there at the behest of the shady group who owned the club to stop any patrons from actually having sex in a place that, true to 70s excess, featured a live sex show and adult films. Frank was there to have sex, if he could. JayJay asked Bill to fast forward the story. It turned out that Frank bought Bill's story of being a gangster. That fascinated him but, even better, Bill knew of a Boston gang that ran a high jacking scheme wherein they'd steal a truckload of goods by luring the driver away with a hooker, then decouple his cab, hook the trailer to another cab, drive it off and sell the contents. It was free money. Bill would do it himself if he only knew where to get a truck and a driver. Frank, as it turned out, did.

The whole operation went smoothly at a truck stop outside a Mississippi river town called Caruthersville, MO. That is it went smoothly until it turned out that the load of cigarettes they stole had already been high-jacked by a gang out of Southern Illinois called the Notorious Shelton Brothers. Frank and Bill had stolen from real gangsters! The Sheltons were not dummies; they had someone watching the truck at the truck stop. It was a simple matter then of taking down the thief's Texas plate number, tracking the truck's owner, threatening that owner with broken legs, and then collecting $6,000 for their troubles.

Frank ended up selling the cigarettes for $2,000, paying the rogue driver $1,000, and borrowing $5,000 to pay back the truck's actual owner, Thomas Franklin of Abilene, Texas. Franklin was not in on the heist, but he got a year's free truck washes out of the fiasco. Bill's take was supposed to be $3,000 which he figured he was owed no matter what. Frank's view was that Bill owed him $3,000 for half of what he what he had to pay Franklin. They "settled" it by agreeing that Bill could work for Frank in Odessa, but Bill refused to accept his pay as part of the $3,000 and Frank never came up with the rest. With Bill's new scheme of sex parties in Odessa, Frank "invested" $3,000, which Bill never paid back, did not accept as the money Frank owned him, and lost anyway when that scheme as well blew up. Whew!

The actual point of Bill's story was short and simple: "I was a bad man in those days, but I was a worse criminal."

145

And I found out that my dad also was a worse criminal than I had known, but I also finally knew how Frank and Freddie met this guy from Boston who seemingly dropped out of the sky and landed in Odessa, Texas. There was not any jealousy between Frank and Bill over Freddie. Frank paid Freddie for sex; Bill did not. But Bill needed money and the Carletons' schemes to Bill's alcohol-addled brain made sense. With Freddie's death and the blow-up with the idiot brothers, Bill left Odessa for New Mexico purgatory but once in Deming he thought long and hard about his life, joined AA, screwed up a couple of times, but finally found the straight and narrow. He never got rich, but better, he got sober. Regrets, he had a few.

"Bill," JayJay asked, "how did Freddie die?"

"She died trying to help me," he said.

He then told a story about the Carleton's party scheme using Juarez girls and how Willie busted the operation. That, of course, led the Carletons to demand to talk to Freddie about what she knew and to ask Bill to retrieve her and bring her to the barn. Bill asserted that Freddie's death was an accident and no good could come of going into the details. But, for his part, he was deeply sorry for his involvement. He loved the gal.

Remorse is a powerful emotion. Two men and a boy felt guilty at not being able to save Freddie: me, her almost ex-husband, and a guy that used and betrayed her, but later discovered that he loved her. Bill argued that he believed that the Carletons were only going to talk to Freddie that night. He made them swear, he said. But anyway, he thought, he could talk them out of anything stupid. Bill's idea was to see if she knew who had busted up the barn, get them to let the girls reschedule, make the money, and return the girls to Juarez. He did not know about the Mexican threats, the turmoil on the south side, or how the two hot heads would actually handle it. After all, he was used to working with professionals.

"Did you kill her?" I asked.

"No, I did not," He replied

"Then why did you run?" asked JayJay.

"Well, the idiots threatened me if I told the cops, but, in truth, I hit bottom in my life. I had fucked up my family...oh, sorry, Bonnie Jay."

"You're fine," JayJay said. "Go on."

"OK, I had ruined my family. Got my friend killed. Saw no future in Odessa and stood a good chance of going to jail. I have always assumed I would someday go to jail. I never figured I'd tell this story to a friend, uh, friends. I figured I'd be telling the cops. You going to turn me in?"

"For what?" she said.

"Accessory to murder, of course."

JayJay looked at me. "Counselor?"

I honestly had not said a word in around 90 minutes.

"From a legal sense, the murder was solved with Cleon's conviction, so don't expect the cops to come knocking. Morally, your story shows that your negative self-assessment is correct, but I think you have paid a high price anyway. If we can reveal the real killer and re-open the case, you might be drawn into it, I guess. I'd suppose you'd get some kind of immunity for testifying. That is just speculation since I am not a criminal lawyer. Of course, it'd be best if you volunteered your story."

147

"That's not happening. Are you going back to Odessa and tell the police what I told you?"

"I know I should, but in all honesty, I don't know if I will."

"Will you call me when you decide?"

"Yes, I will if you accept my apology for being an obnoxious teenager."

A smile. "What other kind is there? Apology accepted."

Chapter 38
By Any Other Name

We slept 'til noon, ate a breakfast/lunch at I-Hop, and headed back to Odessa. JayJay took the backseat to sleep and I drove. Thirty minutes on I-10 and I heard JayJay crying.

"What it is, Baby?"

JayJay had never cried for Freddie. It was part of being hard. Grow up on the south side and people you know die, go away, or disappoint you. "Don't expect nothing from nobody," Freddie advised. She was not gonna be one of those church ladies who went into hysterics when someone passed. Life was hard. Move on. Now she cried.

In my life, I expected success. I expected to do better than my dad. I cried when Freddie died and cried many times after. When it came down to it though, I was a marginal person in her life and all of a sudden my quest to solve her murder seemed like an act of white privilege. I mean, I had the time and money to do it and even if I failed, I could just continue on my path to be a rich lawyer in Odessa, or somewhere else.

I did not share these thoughts with JayJay.

"I think I understand," I said. "Wanna talk about it?"

"Not sure but not now anyway. Do you believe Bill's story? He seemed genuine."

"He was awfully convincing," I admitted. "Like my daddy says, he was as slick as 'cat shit on linoleum.' He talked to us and he did not harm us, so that is a plus."

I thought we were getting a clearer picture. Bill took Freddie to the barn and she died there. How could it be an accident when a knife was in her chest? And which guy did it? Was this just an intellectual exercise, revenge, or as I dream of it, a quest for justice? Was I becoming a vigilante? Damn, life is infinitely messier than a mystery novel.

Chapter 39
House of Ill Repute

Life is indeed messy. As JayJay and I drove through the desert, back in Odessa an impending scandal awaited us. It's not that we had forgotten the racist note that Jack and I had found on my windshield; we had just assumed that my little chat with Dan Gladstone had more or less resolved it. Hardly. Not only had it not been resolved, but whoever had done it had taken on a new tact that not only threatened us, it had potential to kill Jencks and Associates, my relationship to JayJay, and my friendship with the two people, other than JayJay, that I absolutely depended on, Jack and M.A. All this resulted from an anonymous letter to the editor in the *Odessa American* on Sunday, May 21, 1995.

Dear Editor:

I consider it my Christian duty to alert all good Odessans to the moral degeneracy that has invaded our grate city.

Look at America's decline. It is all around us. We see it in the shameful display in race-mixing murder and mayhem in the so-called O.J. Simpson trial. A criminal low-life and his disgusting accomplice occupy the White House, and Slick Willie and the Democrat Congress has already allowed the complete hollowing out of our military. Our boarders are less safe every day, but the Black Caucuses' dreamboat uses tax-payer money to bail out the

Mexicans. And what do the sheep in Odessa do as our Constitutional liberties erode and political correctness undermines our right of free speech? They allow a convicted drug dealer lawyer to live in open sin with a convicted colored wh**e and get rich off the backs of decent folks in West Texas. Wake up, Odessa!

The *American* of course had disclaimers about the veracity of letters to the editors but I had long ago decided never to read that part of the paper because the rants were nasty, badly edited, ungrammatical, and gross exaggerations. Did other Odessans feel the same? But, here's the problem, at least when it came to the reference to me as a drug dealer, I am afraid it was in part based on fact. If somehow it was also true of JayJay, I would be devastated. If even a small part of Odessa believed it, it could hurt our business. And if the Jencks' Associates felt that I had lied to them by not telling my past, we might not even have a business.

The offending letter was not hard for JayJay and me to find. It had been carefully clipped from the newspaper and taped to our front door. Assault by innuendo is a time-honored tradition in American politics and JayJay and I had just become combatants in West Texas' culture war. Before we could go into battle though, we had to revisit times in our lives that we'd rather forget. As a gentleman, I offered to tell my story first.

"Mine's a little bit true, but don't worry, I was never a prostitute," JayJay offered.

"Of course not," I countered.

152

"Don't say 'of course' because people do extreme things to survive, but I never, not in my darkest days, got that desperate. But after Freddie died, I really got scared and really felt trapped."

She also got arrested.

We had never talked about the period right after Freddie died. Freddie had been JayJay's protector from a dysfunctional family, but she had also helped JayJay financially. No, J was not a working girl, but sometimes she worked. She answered the phones many times. She called girls to tell them where to go for outcalls. Once, late at night, Freddie was out, she got hold of Willie Gumble to go pick up a distressed woman from her own home as her angry husband banged on her bedroom door. Since JayJay as much as lived with Freddie, she was pulled into that life on occasion. Freddie helped JayJay with spending money, but never even worried about J's moral fiber. JayJay was an upright citizen.

That changed briefly after Freddie's death. While Freddie had died, the women who worked for her had lived, and they still had the need for money and protection. JayJay already had the key to Freddie's house and Cleon had no claim to it since it was a rental. Freddie's name was on the lease, Freddie said. JayJay had on many occasions taken cash Freddie put in an envelope (Freddie paid cash for everything) to S&S Realty on Old Dixie. Freddie died in late March and JayJay just had a couple of months before summer vacation, so JayJay decided that she, at 17, would continue to live in Freddie's house, pay the rent, and help the girls. And make a little money herself. Freddie had always made enough money to cover rent and groceries. Why not JayJay, she thought? How hard could it be?

She had a lot to learn. Freddie had no records. No list of girls. No client list. No price list. No rules and regulations. It was all in her head. JayJay knew how to answer the phone. That's it. Fortunately, at least JayJay thought it was fortunate, some of the girls called in to see if anything was going on. Were there any calls for their services? JayJay didn't know if they ever called during the day, but several calls came in at night. JayJay could do her homework, take calls, and, in her neat hand-writing, list the first names and phone numbers of the girls who were available to work. Smokey, Tami, Jasmine, etc. were anxious to work and, sure enough, the very first Friday night after Freddie died men called for "visits" at local motels. JayJay didn't know what her take would be from a call, but soon enough she discovered that she took in almost half of a $50 call.

The girl would go on a date. She would get a ride or drive her own car, do her thing and if no problems arose, she'd get the money, put it in an envelope, and drop it at Fatman's BBQ. Smokey, or whoever, would keep $25, Laverne, Fat's wife, would take $5, and Freddie would take $20. JayJay had to learn about the split and the drop from Smokey. She had no idea that Laverne was involved, but she soon learned that even Fatman himself did not know she was. We all do what we have to do to survive.

JayJay's life of crime did not last long enough to learn all the tricks. She did not even discover that others would have had to be paid off: the night clerk at the Sand's motel; a doctor who'd help if a girl got hurt; a dirty cop who

154

wanted extracurricular services not to be too nosy at the Golden Hotel; and, of course, the lawyer to call if things went awry. Come to think of it, Freddie had not even planned for the lawyer contingency, but then she had never had to deal with it. JayJay did.

In early June 1979, JayJay had already found that she needed to do more than answer the phone to make her money. It would start with a phone call all right, but one girl would need to borrow Freddie's car. Another girl had to cancel after first accepting a date, so JayJay needed to track down a substitute. And one time, Lena, after JayJay called her to go on date, knocked on Freddie's/JayJay's door to say that she was too "messed up" to drive her own car over to the Sand's to meet a customer. Would JayJay drive her over? JayJay had never considered she'd have to do such a thing, but then she had a license and she knew how to drive. She would not have to go in and Lena told her that most times she finished her business in less than thirty minutes, so JayJay could just stay in the car and wait for her. She didn't want to wait, but Lena promised her that she would get out as fast as possible and if JayJay felt nervous, she could drive around the block a couple of times and look for Lena out by the back entrance to the Sand's. She'd wait inside the door, close to unit 156, where she was meeting her date. Reluctantly, JayJay agreed.

Another thing that JayJay did not know was that every so often, police departments decide to crack down on prostitution. Usually, citizens' complaints would be too numerous to ignore or prostitutes would get too bold or too obvious. Or maybe a politician, once an Odessa mayor, would be implicated in an arrest and eventually the cops would make a few busts, get a few headlines, and all would go on about their merry way. Odessa in 1979 was already on its way to being called the "Murder Capital of the USA" so the police usually did not worry very much about a little slap and tickle. They would, however, occasionally crack down even if the revelation embarrassed the good citizens that, yes, their husbands and brothers also sometimes took a walk on the wild side.

In June 1979, Lena walked into a set-up; JayJay was observed dropping her off and waiting for her; and both were arrested for soliciting. They were held over one night, released, pleaded no contest, fined $100 each (which JayJay paid in cash), and thus saddled with a criminal record. JayJay, as a minor, was warned about the dangers of a life of crime and told that this time this would not actually go on her permanent record, but the Judge admonished her that he had better never see her in his courtroom again. That ended JayJay's days as a madam, forced her back into her own home, led her to look for a ticket out of there, and resulted in her finding that ticket in Charles Quarles, a very smart boy who didn't have a clue. She married the guy.

"Covey, whoever wrote that letter, has to be with the Odessa police. My record was supposed to be expunged if, by 21, I never got in trouble again. That is what Judge Milburn promised me. Only a cop would know about it and probably a cop who was on duty in 1979."

JayJay did not ask for forgiveness. She probably would not have even if she had hooked briefly, but that was so not JayJay. I should never have worried. I briefly wondered what I would have said if she had indeed gone on dates and, yes, it would have mattered, even if what you do at 17 doesn't really count. In some minds, it does. But under the circumstances, I was relieved to know the story and I did not care at all that she had managed girls at 17. Besides, just a few months later when I was also 17, I got arrested in Sherman, Texas, on an "intent to sell" charge while I was a student at Austin College.

    Talk about a coincidence.

Chapter 40
Roo Fever

I graduated high school at 17. I felt like a man and was proud of what I had accomplished. Second in my graduating class at Permian and 1450 on my SAT were good enough to get me scholarship offers. I looked at a number of schools. UT, Austin, was too big. MacMurray over in Abilene was too close. Sul Ross and Texas Tech were too cowboy. One of my OHS friends, a smart guy, had attended a place I knew nothing about and few of my friends had ever heard of it. It was called Austin College, but guess what? It was not in Austin. It is/was in Sherman, Texas, a place you get to from West Texas by turning left at Dallas and heading north to the Red River. Yes, that Red River. My friend Danny told me that classes were small, the instructors were good, and they had a professor there named Dr. Kenneth Street who could get you into law school. Students there called him Dr. God and if you could pass his Con Law class, you could definitely make it in Law School.

Now, I knew nothing about the difference between state universities and private schools except that state schools were cheaper and had more famous, and presumably better, football teams. The cheaper part was what interested me, but Danny was the first to explain that my grades and scores could probably get me a scholarship. And true enough, I talked with an Admissions guy from Austin College who explained that with a scholarship and a job on campus, I could probably make it-if I kept my grades up around 3.5 or so. I could be an Austin Scholar, whatever that was.

I was interested in being close to Dallas and having money to go, but I did have to convince my mom. As I grew into my teenage years, she was a presence but not a force in my life. She was there, but her life revolved around church and more church. I think she put everything into religion because her marriage was so meaningless and because I was so absorbed with school. She had always come to my sports events but as I drew away from them and became more studious and more alone, she seemed a remote figure in my life. She could care less about my intellectual pursuits. Thus, I was not ready for her determination to dictate my college choice. To her, there were only two places to consider, Hardin-Simmons (in Abilene) and Baylor (in Waco), both Baptist institutions. I could not tell her that I had already begun to think of West Texas fundamentalists as cult worshipers or that I would not consider a West Texas school. Baylor, I would think about.

Lo and behold, my PONY baseball coach saved me from the Baptists. Encountering my mom at Piggly Wiggly, he casually asked her where I intended to go to College. Naturally, her preferences came up, but she told him that I was also thinking of Austin College. "Really?" he said. He had gone to Austin College; his dad had gone to Austin College; and in a couple of years, his first son would go to Austin College. This intrigued my mom, but what sold her were a couple of other things. Austin College was a "church" school, Presbyterian in this case, and its president was, in fact, a Presbyterian minister, Dr. Harry Smith. "Mrs. Jencks, you can be sure, he will be in Christian hands up in

159

Sherman." That convinced my mom; the scholarship convinced me; and now I just had one hurdle to overcome. Could I really go to a place whose mascot was a Kangaroo? In the end, I could.

What I did not expect was Animal House.

Chapter 41
Knock, Knock, Knockin' At My Door

The College looked every bit a church school. Tree-lined sidewalks, staid brown buildings, and a prominent Chapel across from the Administration building as if they were co-equals in the education of eager young adults. Live Oak trees lined the main walkway and stood testament to a college atmosphere. Dang, they even had a pretty decent football team with a famous All American, Larry Kramer, who had played tackle at big-time Nebraska. And pretty girls? We were in Texas, no? I admired it a lot on sight and even more when the skinny older man who helped me unload my stuff to take it into my dorm turned out to be the president himself. Wow, I like this college stuff.

Then the sun went down. My dorm, Luckett, named after some old dead white guy, looked like a military bunker but, in truth, it was more like a fraternity house at Dartmouth. Except the only qualification for belonging to it was to be assigned a room there. We did meet a resident director, talk to a few student mentors, and get a rundown on rules but then Led Zeppelin cranked up, margaritas flowed, girls dropped by, and weed was consumed. The first night of the first day of the rest of my life!

My roomie was a football player from East Texas, Big Sandy. He was not that huge, but he was intense. Bear we called him. In the Teacher Program, he said. Gonna be a coach, he knew. If he didn't kill Coach Kramer before two-a-days were over.

"You an Austin Scholar?"

"Yeah," I said.

"Great, you can write my Heritage of Western Culture papers," he said.

"No fucking way," I said.

"OK, cool, just edit them."

The geniuses who paired Bear and me must have looked at it this way. Two males, both with football in their backgrounds, one from West Texas, one from East Texas. Perfect fit! At first, I thought they must have been smoking the bad weed from down on "the block" in East Sherman and not the good stuff coming up from Dallas but darned if the match was not made in heaven. I understood what he was and where he came from. He was almost never there. He had no girlfriend to bring in for sex. He drank to excess elsewhere, came in late, and fell asleep before his head hit the pillow. Perfect roommate. His only request: leave the door unlocked so he never had to look for his keys.

That was my downfall.

I had a professor at AC who once said: you are always punished for your best qualities, not your worst. In my case my trusting disposition, study habits, and cooperative attitude meant that I was often in the library, the door was open, and my car keys were accessible. Now the truth is that I was not a party animal or a big drinker. In all of high school, I doubt if I drank as much as a twelve-pack of beer. I did not change my habits much in college because to maintain a 3.5 at Austin College looked daunting. My Freshman Biology class under Jack Pierce was full of pre-meds who all knew of the college's reputation for cranking out future doctors. A third of them seemed to have emptied out the Indian subcontinent. My classes in American

162

History and Political Science had professors who were already legends (Ed Phillips and Ken Street), and my English prof, Carol Daeley, seemed to know as much about politics as Street and threw in Asian literature in translation to boot. Three out of four of these expected students to talk as well as take notes and Pierce expected us to know every single detail of every single topic every time. I made 73 on my first Biology test and felt devastated until I found out that the class average was 70. Then I found out there would be no curve. Hopkins Library, here I come.

On one Saturday late in October, I was feeling pretty good about things. I had taken two exams on Friday, a Ken Street multiple choice exam that amazingly I had finished and a Biology test that I could envision making an 80 on. Bear was on a football road trip, so I might be able to grab dinner at Slater's cafeteria and come to the Luckett lobby to watch color TV in complete quiet. It all worked out but I fell asleep watching TV and no one was around to wake me up. That is until about 9:00 PM when someone shook my shoulders and yelled, "Wake up, Covey Jencks, wake your ass up!" I think I was dreaming about football at Permian because the voice sounded familiar. Dang, is that my old teammate, Bo Gladstone? It was. Bo had "dropped in" on his way from Dallas to get back to school where he was playing football at Central Oklahoma University.

I don't recall much about Bo's visit except his gnarly attitude and what happened later in the evening. Bo drilled me on why I had chosen to go to a liberal college and my attempts to explain what a Liberal Arts institution really was fell on deaf ears. I think at some point I "reassured" him that AC also had some racists and Reaganites. When I told him that I was taking Biology, he laughed and recalled that once he had made a higher grade on a high school Biology test than I had. You know, the one he stole in advance and threatened to beat me up if I didn't give him the answers for it? By this time, I wanted to be rid of Bo and hit the rack. I told him so but he said he wanted to see my room. He had come to the conclusion that Central Oklahoma was a much better school than AC since it "took care" of its football players and the athletic dorm was much nicer than "this dump." By this time, I loved my dump.

I reluctantly took Bo to my room. He laughed derisively that I had brought my old "portable" TV from home, the one that weighed about 40 pounds and was not equipped for color. He sneered at the papers and books on my side of the room. He admired Bear's Big Sandy's current football schedule haphazardly scotch taped to the wall over his bed. I had had about enough and was about to ask him to leave when the campus police banged on my door. "Open up. Dorm inspection." Sure enough, I opened the door and there was security guard, Officer Larry, standing there with two of Sherman's finest. They went straight to my dresser, opened the sock drawer, and pulled out a plastic bag with well more than two ounces of marijuana. It looked like it had just been thrown in there because, well, it had. Off I went to the police department in downtown Sherman on Travis Street.

My Toyota Corolla, the one with Austin College emblazoned on the bumper and my tags clearly visible, was observed leaving a Dallas establishment on Greenville Avenue that was well known for drug deals. The Dallas cops traced the tags to me and called the Sherman

164

constabulary to "scare" the college kids who seemed to be flocking to Dallas to buy weed. Austin College had come up in numerous reports but, really, not nearly as many as SMU. Still, one of the narcs knew AC and a little dose of scaring us straight might set us on a better path. The one little problem was that I did not do it and I had not been in Dallas at all that weekend. My car had. Whoever took my car to Dallas must have decided they had been nailed, so they drove it back to the lot, put the weed in my dresser, and melted away. I can imagine their convulsions of laughter when they saw me sound asleep on the Luckett couch.

Unlike JayJay, I had resources at my disposal even though I was unaware. Officer Larry knew me and believed my story. He also knew a lawyer from downtown Sherman who was willing to help college kids for free who were hassled by the Sherman cops. His name was Roger Sanders and his intervention saved the day. He got me out. He pleaded my case. He argued that the cops in Dallas had not seen me, only my car, and the cops in Sherman did not have a warrant to search my dorm. I was not given the opportunity to request a lawyer. In fact, no part of the Constitution seemed to be involved in anything that happened to me that October night. The charges were dropped (so I was not a convicted drug dealer); I made a friend for life; and never again did I leave my keys on my desk with the door unlocked. Austin College then had to set up protocols for dealing with Sherman's finest and that resulted in AC's establishing its own police force and eventually Officer Larry became Chief Larry. I also worked for Roger Sanders for free for the rest of my college career at my insistence to pay back what I owed him.

How this incident could come up sixteen years later with only one-half of the story told could only be explained by my Odessa visitor that night. That is the guy I almost forgot had been there when the cops knocked on my door.

My old friend, Bo Gladstone, brother of Dan, the officer who found Freddie's body.

Chapter 42
Two for the Price of One

"JayJay, we are working on two crimes, not one," I said.

"Tell me about that and tell me how it helps us with the Letter to the Editor."

"The first is easier. I have been thinking about your situation back in the day when Freddie died, and you became Madame Black Butterfly."

"Funny, ha, ha. What about it?" she asked.

"You said that you learned after the fact that other parties had to be paid off, like the cop who was paid not to hassle your girls at the Golden Hotel. Who was that?

"I don't know, but I see where you're coming from."

"Would Willie know?" I wondered.

"If anyone alive knows, it'd be Willie. Delicious irony, no? Angry black man paying off Redneck cop."

"Yep, I am thinking Dan Gladstone," I said.

"That really makes sense, so that would explain why he might try to scare us off or run us out of town. I bet he is still dirty as can be."

"Maybe, and his little brother Bo may not be any cleaner. Of course, it could just be their hatred working. But, wow, they are awful at disguising their involvement. Really awful."

"We can look into that. I will talk to Mr. Willie again. What about the letter?" she asked.

"I have thought about it. Shall we demand a retraction? Write a rebuttal? Ignore it?

"No," she said, "we have to respond but not in kind. You know my cousin who's a Social Security Manager up in Dallas?"

"Hmmm, vaguely, yeah. Her name is Janelle or something?"

"Right, she told me that when she became a District Manager, they sent her to South Carolina, to a university, I think, to learn how to deal with the media. One thing you never do is respond by direct reference to what some crackpot has alleged. Like, 'No, I did not steal that money.' By doing so, you automatically link yourself to theft."

"So, what do you do?" I asked.

"Issue a statement that the SSA cannot account for certain funds but you are making every effort to locate either the funds or the person or persons responsible for it."

"I see. Clever. So how does this relate to us?"

"No denial. No acknowledgment. No panic, but..."

"But what?"

"Covey, the *American* sometimes does Sunday fluff pieces on local celebrities. There is going to be one on me and my lawyer boyfriend. It will be called 'Odessa's New Power Couple in Black and White, '" she said.

"No!"

"Yep, I talked with Shelia VanStavern who writes it and who owns a Toyota. She is upset the *American* even published such a letter, so she needs another column and we might fit. If her editor approves, she wants to cast us in a different light. And, you know I have another play coming up soon, 'The Taming of the Shrew.' The article will be good promotion and I look forward to playing a bad girl."

Man, did I love this bad girl. I know there'd be no taming her. We might become Odessa's new power couple, but was a racist cop out to stop us? And what role did he have in the 1979 murder, if any?

Chapter 43
News Not Fit to Print

I guess I do worry a lot. When I read the letter to the editor, I thought the shit would hit the fan. A few days later, I was beginning to ask, what shit, what fan?

I made sure to be at Jencks and Associates the day after it appeared. As usual, Alberto was there and working. He asked how Deming was, half listened that we found our man, and said: "That's cool." M.A. arrived an hour later and I know men should not always focus on what women are wearing but...OK, no comment, but Debra Winger at Gilley's in *Urban Cowboy* would be jealous. Jack was in Abilene and Erica was in class. Just before noon, I casually asked the other two:

"Say, did anybody see that letter in the *American* yesterday?"

"Which one?" asked Alberto?

"About the lawyer, you know?"

"Sure, that had to be about Tony Blanco and his defense of drug dealers. But his wife is Latina, a brown one."

"No, no," chipped in M.A. "That has to be Mike Phillips, the guy who was disbarred for helping his brother with a meth lab."

"Oh, you didn't think of JayJay and me?"

They both laughed.

"Yeah, sure, Mr. Goody Two Shoes and Miss Black America. Well, you do fit the livin' in sin part, but since when is that real news in 1995?" asked M.A.

I waited for the outraged phone calls or press inquiries until about 3:00 and then went home. Maybe the letter would not come back to haunt us.

But then- will whoever is doing this just have to come up with a better line of attack? The answer to this question seemed pretty obvious.

Chapter 44
The Hip Bone is Connected to the...

When I am in one place, I often think of what is happening at the same moment in another place I used to be. Like, when I walked to work in D.C., I often saw this seemingly homeless guy playing chess with multiple persons near the fountain in DuPont Circle. I saw countless persons get up and walk away from his games with defeated looks on their faces. Is that still going on? Or, is some freshman in my old dorm room at Luckett finally settling into the pace of college life? Or flunking out? Who is wearing number 63 for Permian this year? They are very good again and will soon play another powerhouse, Converse Judson, I think, for the state championship. Does that guy start? Is he a good student? Why do I care?

I think I care because I am fascinated by connections, my connections, in life. Our shared connections and shared patterns must result in similar outcomes and similar life lessons, no? Or not, I guess, depending on parents, experiences, and mental capacities. Useless thoughts really, but what about the Gladstone boys? We had so many connections and shared patterns, but we simply did not see the world in the same way. We grew up in the same town, played the same games, went to the same schools, had the same friends, had the same kind of uneducated, racist parents, and dated the same girls.

The similarities no doubt did not end there, but in the end the differences became the defining connection. Why had they grown from being mere schoolyard bullies to being potentially dangerous criminals? Why had I not taken my own father's path and used my brain to cheat people for personal profit? Why didn't I find comfort in a worldview that saw other races as inferior or threatening to me? Why did I insist on simply seeing them as other humans? I knew that nothing could happen in the culture that could change my mind about people with all their mixed-up cultural influences and histories, so I assumed nothing anyone could ever say or do would change the Gladstones' views. Like Junior Baker said, let them have their prejudices, but hold them accountable for their actions. How many people out there are various combinations of my view and the Gladstones' and will we ever, as a society, simply have to choose to act on their views or mine? The events of the last several years left no doubt in mind that many issues in U.S. society remain despite the laws and programs that were put in place in the 60s and 70s. Yet, those seem so long ago.

The other thought I had was also simple. One action leads to another. As my prof said, you can't act like something you did never happened. Moving back to Odessa led to a series of events. Freddie's death led to many different events. I was convinced that the Gladstones did something in 1979 that led to actions in 1993-95 that would inevitably lead to events in 1995 and 1996. And maybe they, or one of them at least, had done other things as well. That must mean that something else was bound to happen and JayJay and I were part of the pattern that Dan and Bo were designing. Oddly enough, JayJay and I were dealing with two sets of idiot brothers and I could not decide which set was more dangerous. Clearly, the set that lived in the same town posed the proximate danger but the set that included the probable murderer might pose the ultimate danger.

The dilemma really came down to the same question. Who would act first, them or me?

I decided that JayJay and I had to initiate the next chain reaction and I hoped that our connections would trump theirs, whoever *they* might be.

Chapter 45
Let the Game Begin

"We are missing something," JayJay said. "What connects the Carletons to the Gladstones? Or, are they disconnected?"

"Hard to see how they could be disconnected," I said, "but back in the day athletes and non-athletes seemed to run in different circles."

"Yes, in school, but after we left school, folks were divided into who stayed in Odessa and who left. You, Liberal Boy, went packing," she said.

"Apply that to 1979 and that means the two older boys, Delbert Carleton and Dan Gladstone were two guys out of school who stayed or at least came back, to Odessa and Bo and Aaron were still in school, Bo at Permian and Aaron at OC,." I said.

She added: "Yes, and one was a cop and the other was a wannabe criminal."

"Right, and the criminal wanted to hold a party at the Golden Hotel that perhaps the cop would help with for the right price or the right incentive."

"But we don't know if the Carletons knew they needed that protection," she said.

"Shall we just assume it?"

"What would it prove?" she asked.

"That Gladstone lost his pay off and that both the Carletons and the Gladstones hold secrets on the other that could be used to undo them."

"So," JayJay concluded, "we come along trying to discover who killed Freddie but that leads to knowledge that Dan probably covered up the parties and maybe the murder!"

"Right, and now the Odessa brother team wants to scare us off the investigation and ..."

"And the other brother team probably knows from the Odessa idiots that we are snooping around," she said.

"The bad news then is that we are likely in danger from both sets," I responded.

"The good news?"

"They are still idiots and hotheads...except maybe for Delbert."

"I like this," she said, "so the obvious strategy is to divide the Odessa hotheads and isolate the other, smarter one?"

"No doubt," I said.

Chapter 46
The Winkte

I knew that I had to enlist M.A.'s help. The idea was to work one of the Gladstones off against the other and that required more information. M.A. had already found probable locations for Aaron and Delbert, Jr., but I had to be sure the people she found were the right persons Then, once found, I had to plot a strategy for dealing with them individually. Ideally, I needed to make contact with each without their knowing what I was up to. M.A., I believed could do her computer magic and help me the most. First, though, I had to figure out why she was sitting at her desk dressed as a Native American man.

"Good morning, M.A.," I said, trying my best to seem casual.

"Go ahead, Boss, you can ask."

Her hair was braided and pulled back in ponytails on both sides. She wore a man's western shirt, a leather vest, a long bone necklace with a half-moon hanging well below where her breasts used to be, and large flat silver earrings peeping out from her hair.

"Ok, why no war paint?" I asked.

"This is not a warrior's dress. This is simply a Comanche's daily wear for one of the berdache."

"I don't speak Comanche."

"Good, because the word is French. When the westerners encountered the Plains Indians, they found that there were not two sexes, there were three. Some persons had the genitalia of a man or a woman, but they preferred to

177

dress and like the opposite gender. They were a third gender, so eventually, the French term "berdache" for the younger person in a gay relationship came to be their collective name. After that, the term 'winkte' or 'two spirts' came to be used and such persons were often said to possess magical or healing powers."

"Do tell," I said, "and you honor the winkte today because?"

"Oh, it's Western Week at OHS and I always honor that. First time you ever commented though and that's cool."

"Well, don't think I don't notice."

"That's fine, Boss. I also want to remind Beth that I swing both ways so she better behave herself."

"Moving on," I quickly said, "I want to get back to you about the Carletons."

"What do you want to know about them?" I asked.

"You mean besides their addresses and phone numbers? Yes, I know more about Aaron, but I am learning about Delbert, too."

I quickly responded: 'Wait a minute now, we have to be discrete. So, we can't be asking about them all over town."

"Covey, this isn't Mayberry and folks don't get their information down at Floyd's barber shop anymore."

"Enlighten me."

"All right, now I am not sure about the ethics of all this, OK? So, I know it's going to sound strange. But I have been talking to Aaron Carleton on AOL at night for about two weeks."

"AOL???"

"America On-Line."

"I know what it stands for, but he can't know we are gathering information on him," I said.

"Right, and he has no idea. Ever heard of a chat room?"

"No, can't say that I have," I said.

"People can go into them with rooms AOL has set up, or ones' people have set up themselves, or just privately. It's mostly for sex talk as I have discovered. The good thing is that you never use your real name or initials unless, of course, you are an idiot."

"I get it, so he uses Aaron."

"Almost. He is ACnMK."

"And you are?" I added.

"OK, here is where ethics come into it. I am 'Wyld Gurl,' 'Dr. Love,' or 'Dessa Chica.' Cute, huh? And there's nothing to link it to the real me."

"You have three names?"

"I just use one at a time, but I have a profile for each and as far as he knows, I am either a single twenty-five-year-old hottie, a male professor, or an Odessa Latina."

"Why?" I asked.

"Each one can have a conversation with him about different things. He is hooked on chatting and he seems never to notice that these three are never on at the same time."

"And you are sure this is our guy?"

"One hundred percent positive," she assured me.

"Any other ethical issues, I need to worry about?"

"You don't really care about computer sex, do you?" she asked.

"No, that is Beth's worry, not mine. Give me what you know. This is hard to believe."

"I know you can learn almost anything from anyone online if you work hard enough or lie beautifully."

"OK, go!" I encouraged her.

"He is married with two kids. Has not slept with the little woman in over six months…"

"M.A.!"

"OK, OK. He hates his brother and has not talked to him in over 15 years. He does know that Delbert lives in the Dallas area and cheats people for a living. He works at a Trailer Supply and Repair Company. He misses Odessa and won't say why he left and won't say why he can't come back, even if Dessa Chica says he would blow his pipes if he did."

"You learned all this?"

"Oh, and much more, Boss."

"How much time do you spend on this?"

"Next question, please."

"All right, Dessa needs to get one more piece of intel, OK?"

"Oh, she is good at what she does, so shoot."

I added: "She needs to find out if ACnWF knows one Dan Gladstone in Odessa who seemingly does not like anyone from the south side-where I am sure Dessa lives."

"Claro, boss, claro."

"And let me know as soon as she knows, OK, Winkte?"

180

Chapter 47
Chat Me Up

Dessa Chica: Hey, AC, what you doin'?

ACnWF: Hi, Chica, how's the Big O?

Dessa Chica: Same ole, same ole. Unhappy little Latina tonight.

ACnMK: What's up, Buttercup? Want me to kiss it?

Dessa Chica: Not tonight, mi amor. Muy triste esta noche.

ACnMK: Don't speak Mexican, OK?

Dessa Chica: Oh, sorry. Habit. I had a bad situation tday and may be in trouble with the cops.

ACnMK: lol, you disburbin' the peace in Odessa?

Dessa Chica: This asshole cop came to the house lookin' for my older brother. I haven't seen that sucker in like three months, but the cop would not believe me. He told me that he was going to haul me in or turn me over to INS. Hell, I was born in Odessa. I don't know what my brother does with his time.

ACnMK: You get the guy's name? I know some cops out there.

Dessa Chica: He said his name but I dunno. Dan somethin'.

ACnMK: Gladstone?

Dessa Chica: LOL, yeah, I was gonna say Gallstone.

ACnMK: Want me to give him a call?

Dessa Chica: For real? I thought you have not lived here in like 20 years.

ACnMK: 16 but I stay in touch with some folks. Dan is one of them.

Dessa Chica: He was not nice, not nice at all.

ACnMK: Hey, baby, be sweet to him and maybe it'll work out. He likes the young ones.

Dessa Chica: You know what, I'd better go. Usted dos suena enfermo en la cabeza. Disfruta del infiero. (You are nuts. Die in hell.)

Chapter 48
Police Matters

"That settles that," I said. "Dan was in on it and at least Aaron knows that we are snooping around."

"Covey, how stupid is this guy?" asked JayJay, "How dangerous was it for M.A. to call him a sicko, even in Spanish? I gotta believe that we need to go to the authorities now."

"To say what exactly? That we have new suspicions about a murder they feel was solved long ago or to say that we have acquired new information through completely unethical means that two men know each other? We need hard evidence. Or a new crime? An even then, do we trust the Odessa police? I have lots of questions!"

"Point taken. If Gladstone is dirty, how could he have gone this long undiscovered?"

"I think it's time to talk with Junior Baker again, don't you?" I asked.

Looking back at our investigation now, I realize that over and over I made assumptions or drew conclusions based on limited perspective or incomplete knowledge. My negative assessment of the Odessa Police drew from tales I had heard, interactions my own father had, and, of course, my own prejudices derived from personal experiences with the Sherman Police. I did not know of the ups and downs of the Odessa Police Department (OPD), the number of conflicts between a series of Chiefs and the City Council, the various times the community had discovered problems due to lack of supervision of rogue cops, or the new development that occurred just prior to my return to Odessa-the Creation of an Odessa Police Community Relations Department that, I suspected, came in part from the repercussions from the Lozano case. Then and now, it seems, that outreach programs would crop up to try to avoid the problems that I now knew to exist in the 1970s. Junior Baker in part set me straight.

"Dan Gladstone? Dirty? I guess that would not surprise me. I am not aware of any formal charges, but I do know that he has not gone up in the ranks in 15 years. That's almost unheard of. He must be 51 or 52 and he'd be eligible to collect a pension after 20 years of service and reaching the age of 50, so, assuming that he joined the force at age 32, maybe 1996 or 1997 might be crucial twenty-year service date for him. It's getting mighty close for him to earn free money. The truth is back in the 70s the OPD did not have the supervision they needed and some bad apples also took advantage of vulnerable populations, like folks on the south side."

"How about payoffs?" I asked.

"It happens. Frankly, things were a bit of turmoil then. That's why I left in part. It is much better now, though no place is perfect. Look at L.A."

"How did you know he joined the force at 32?"

Baker smiled, "Because I hired him at a time we needed warm bodies and he had served in Viet Nam."

So, my timing was perfect. I was kicking up dust about a sixteen-year-old case that would threaten one guy's pension and two others' normal lives who, as far as I knew, had committed no crimes since. Why not let sleeping dogs lie? Well, because it's not right and because I doubt very seriously that there had been any personality or behavior change in any of the idiots. Besides, with the notes and the letter to the editor, they are probably going to ratchet up their warnings a serious notch or two in the very short while. We had to be very careful.

We weren't the only ones.

Chapter 49
What Would Hitchcock Do?

"Former Odessan Murdered in Frisco" read the *Odessa American* headline on page 3.

"Delbert Carleton, Jr., oldest child of Delbert Carleton, Sr., prominent Odessa rancher and oil man of the early-to-mid-Twentieth Century found murdered in his car outside of his beautiful Frisco, Texas home. Robbery suspected. Mr. Carleton is survived by his wife, Cecelia, his twin boys Raymond and Daymond (ages, 9), his brother Aaron of McKinney, and his sister, Candice of Dallas. Mr. Carleton's successful real estate business in North Texas has played a key role in the area's boom."

A subsequent Erica visit to the Ector County Library to copy articles from the *Dallas Morning News* provided new information and corrected some. Delbert was found shot in the head in his driveway in Frisco at 6:30 PM on Tuesday, January 6, 1996. His wallet and his watch were stolen, but no one heard a shot or saw a suspect. The police had no leads. Delbert did not own the real estate company, North Texas Realty; he just worked for it.

No one was calling it an execution, but that's what it looked like to me, and in a quick call to Junior Baker, he agreed. He also suggested the use of a silencer and noted the fact that Delbert may have known his assailant since there is no mention of a struggle and he'd bet his bottom dollar that Delbert's window had been lowered. He knew his assailant.

"Aaron," I thought!

JayJay partially agreed but also demurred.

"We know that he is an idiot, but this would take idiocy to a new level," she said. "Even a cursory investigation into their relationship would reveal that they were estranged. He's an obvious suspect.

"I wonder if M.A. knows anything from Aaron?" I asked.

"How?" she asked.

"I hope she doesn't but maybe through that AOL business."

I called her and when we finished I had new concerns and a new hypothesis.

"Hello, M.A, how are you tonight?"

"What is it, Boss?"

"OK, straight to it then. Have you talked with Aaron Carleton on AOL again?"

"No, but funny you should ask."

"Why is it funny?"

"I went on the night before last, let's see Tuesday after work, to check email, and I just decided to check my other identities. I went on a Dessa Chica, Dr. Love, and Wyld Gurl, all in a row."

"Yeah?"

"On every one of the Aaron, popped up to say hello."

"I did not answer to any of them, but it seemed odd for him almost to be lurking."

"Roughly what time after work was this?" I asked.

"Say 6:00 PM and after."

"Thanks, M.A."

"Covey, did you want me to try to get more information?"

"You just did. In fact, it is critical information. Many thanks."

I put down the phone and yelled to JayJay.

"Get an overnight bag. We are getting out of here."

I guess the tone of my voice conveyed that this was not an arbitrary suggestion. I had reason behind it. She grabbed her stuff and I grabbed mine. I left the light on in the living room and we jumped in the Camry and took off.

"What is it, Covey?"

"*Strangers on a Train*, but this time it's not strangers."

"Please talk in English and not in movies, OK, Covey Jencks?"

I explained that in *Strangers Meet on a Train* two men collaborate on committing the perfect murder by suggesting each could kill a person the other wanted dead at a pre-arranged time, thus allowing the partner to concoct an iron-clad alibi. Aaron was doing just that in having multiple conversations at the time of Delbert's killing. My theory was that Dan Gladstone killed Delbert Carleton and thus Aaron Carleton would be looking to kill us. That way Aaron's fear that his brother would give him up and Dan's fear that we'd expose him would be addressed and both parties could be seen and encountered by multiple persons at the time of the other's murderous act. Then that person would be home free. We were probably next.

"And what about Bill O'Toole?"

"That's right! I owe him a call anyway. Then we will plan our next step."

It took a couple of tries to reach him, but when I did, Bill was unaware of Delbert's death. He was also not concerned.

"I doubt if that knucklehead Aaron even knows where I am. If he comes this way, though, he'll receive a rude welcome. It's either him or me and I guess I am ready for him. That goes for the other fellow, too, but then I didn't have a big fight with them boys and I have not been rooting around investigating. I think you are in greater danger than me."

I had to agree to that.

Chapter 50
On the Lam

I called Jack to let him know that I had to go on indefinite leave. He'd be in charge of the office. Thankfully he accepted that and did not reply, "So, what else is new?" Instead, he said something that made sense to me, but I did not have time to take it in fully.

"Covey, you know that we are all pulling for you in this investigation and you can call on any of us at any time."

"Thanks, Jack. Is M.A. keeping all of you up to date?"

"Next to the Cowboys, it's all we talk about that the water cooler."

"Funny since we don't have a water cooler."

"One thing bothers me about the story, Boss."

"Yeah?"

"Unless I missed something almost everything you know about Wild Bill, you learned directly from him. Maybe a little from Beth."

"Hmm, that is just about right, I guess. Why?"

"What makes you think he's a reliable source? He might have lied to you. He probably lied to Beth, too. Besides, family narratives are rarely totally accurate."

"Damn, that's scary. You and M.A. want to look into his background more? Maybe there's something else. You know honestly, we have wondered all along if Bill was leveling with us, but he seemed so ready and easy to talk to. You are right, get on it."

"Sure, I'll get M.A. to trace his Boston background and once I finish the brief I am doing for Ranger vs. Long Range Haulers, I will do what I can."

I hated to waste any of their time, but I suspected that, as usual, Jack was right at least in part, about the info on Bill. I was sure he never told me the total truth, but does it clarify our search for a murderer? I liked my current theory of the investigation, the *Strangers on a Train*.

"OK, and if we have to reach you?"

"I'll call in."

"Yeah, I guess you don't have a cell phone yet, right?"

"No, aren't those are only for drug dealers?"

"That's beepers and pagers, Covey. We can talk but I suggest you stop by Radio Shack and get a Nokia 9000."

"Sure, buddy, first thing."

"Boss, that's an order!" he almost shouted.

"Yes, sir, I am on it!"

"And give me the number!"

"Geez, no directory?" I wondered.

"No 411 for cell phones and no crank calls. Call me!"

"Will do."

Chapter 51
Hiding in Plain Sight

Our plan was to return to the Suites Motel where I first lived, pay cash, and check in under the name Archie Leach. Using Cary Grant's real name, I thought, was a nice touch. The clerk one-upped me though.

"And your companion is Miss Hepburn, I assume?"

"Yes."

"Audrey or Katherine?"

"Shhh, she is disguising herself as Miss Black America."

It was a light moment in an otherwise scary time. Delbert's death ended the walk down memory lane. To this point, our investigation was mostly an intellectual exercise and, dare I say it, a bonding opportunity. JayJay and I had been through a lot together, but now there was a very real existential threat. Part of me said that JayJay and I should separate for the time being so that we could not be found, and eliminated, together. The other part of me said that we belonged together come what may. We relied on each other and took care of each other; you know, "until death do we share." It was not marriage; it was something better. As usual, JayJay had the last word: "I'm not going anywhere, Sir Galahad. I am missing none of the action. Besides, I'll probably end up saving your sorry ass."

Breaking news. The thing about Texas is it's big. That meant two things to JayJay and me. If somebody comes hunting for us from McKinney, Texas, he had to come a long way and however one traverses this huge state, it is hard not to be seen. Whoever got Delbert had to be pretty good, but let's see if such a daring act really went unnoticed.

JayJay made a point. Delbert was still dead.

Right, but we now have the advantage of not being surprised. The other reason size makes a difference is that there are many places to hide in this territory if one so chooses. You don't have to go to New Mexico, like Wild Bill. I mean, JayJay and I could simply have gone a few miles north of Odessa to a lovely little town called No Trees (and if you have to ask why it has that name, you have not been paying attention to this story). JayJay and I discussed hiding. She asked all the reasonable questions. For how long? How would we know when to come out? What about her job? Her play? Our sanity? Now really, Covey, isn't it now time to involve the police? She was cool with the move to the Suites, but only to allow us to take stock of the situation.

"Of course, of course," I said. "Let's just get a plan."

So, we did.

Chapter 52
With a Little Help from Our Friends

We would rely on "old school ties" in both Odessa and McKinney to build an early warning system. First, we'd take Willie Gumble up on his offer to help by asking him to shadow JayJay at work and at the Globe rehearsals. He readily agreed though he would need remuneration for his lost revenue "at his other job," whatever that was.

"Let me look at our budget, Willie." Two seconds later. "Agreed."

JayJay weighed in.

"Thank you, Mr. Willie. There is a high fence behind and on both sides of the dealership. I think the two entrances on 8th street are the only access points. There is an observation post in the McDonald's parking lot on the east side or on the dining floor, if you like their coffee"

"Roger that," said Willie.

"The Globe has front and back doors, but the front is manned at all rehearsals. I think the rear is the danger. It should be locked, but some folks go out of it to smoke so it is not secure. Also, I will call your cell when I leave either place."

I looked at her.

"Where did you serve? Desert Storm or FBI?"

"Common sense," Liberal Boy. And street sense."

"I'm impressed."

"Can I go now, Love Birds?" asked Willie.

The other part of the plan was to be proactive. We had to reach out to North Texas. A quick call to the Austin

College Alumni Office revealed what I thought, that an old friend had taken up residence in McKinney. Darwin Petty, the second African-American student body president at AC, was now Associate Dean of Humanities at Colin Community College in fair McKinney. He had acquired a Ph.D. in History at Rice University, taught a while at the University of Houston, become History chair there, and moved into Administration. The escalator was going up. Funny, I thought his greatest talent was doing the Time Warp at the AC Pub in 1982. Odd to find him just down the road from Sherman in 1996, but there he was.

"Covey Jencks? Where you calling from, some public library in D.C.? Solve the contradictions of Human Nature yet?"

"Are you still singing?

"Of course, the college has a stage!"

"Is your German always perfect?"

"Natürlich, mein Freund. Was benötigen Sie?"

"Believe it or not, once again, I seek your wisdom and counsel. That's what I need."

I described my complicated situation and briefly shared the back story. I wanted him to see if he could find Aaron Carleton's home and business addresses, identify the vehicle he drove to work, and check if car was where it was supposed to be every day."

"What about weekends?"

"Uh, those too? If his car is gone at mid-morning either Saturday or Sunday, call me."

"Shall I tuck him in at night?

"No, but it's a thought."

"For how long, Cove?"

195

"Two weeks tops."

"Can I get help?" he asked.

"As in?"

"The beautiful white boy who lives at my house?"

"Geez, Petty, what a Texas cliché! An operatic gay History professor who speaks German. Sure, enlist his help and my Christmas gift this year will be two tickets to the Dallas Philharmonic."

"Accepted, Freund. Take care, Covey."

One last step we had to consider: Should we attempt to beard the lion in his own nest? I am pretty sure that is not a saying, but, still, should we take preemptive action and confront Carleton or, again, alert police whether in McKinney or in Odessa?

JayJay responded: "I am tired of hearing this question, Covey. Please, the only professional law enforcement officer we actually know is Junior Baker. Put our dilemma to him and let's act on his advice."

"Streetwise and wise, wise. Of course, that was just going to be my suggestion."

She added, "And, are you assuming that Dan Gladstone doesn't need watching? That's putting a lot on your movie theory. For that theory to hold any water, the hits have to be pretty close together. Otherwise, one party, or parties, have time to figure it out. Just like you may have already. We need to get cracking."

Note to self. Hold on to this woman.

Chapter 53
A Thin Reed

I admit that I felt that not all the bases were covered. Things got even more complicated when I talked with my new best friend, Junior Baker.

"It seems to be that you have little to share formally with any law enforcement agency. It's pure speculation, "he said.

"I know."

"If you confront Aaron, he denies all and, if he's guilty, you warn him."

"I know."

"No way O'Toole told you the whole story."

"I know."

"And Gladstone has firearms skills and maybe a black heart."

"That about sums it up."

Baker concluded: "No, there is another wild card, Bo Gladstone. I hear that he is about to be investigated for insurance irregularities. He's another cornered rat."

"Wonderful. Any other cheery thoughts?"

"I may have one or two friends both at the Federal level and in Odessa. Let me see what I can find anything about any of the characters in your drama or the murder investigation in Frisco."

"Many thanks, Junior. I am in your debt."

"Yes, and perhaps over your head."

"'And you read minds," I added.

Chapter 54
All I Have to Do is Dream

Aaron Carleton had a gun to JayJay's head as I stood there wordlessly embarrassed that I was only in my jockey shorts. Aaron seemed to be either ascending an escalator at Metro Center in D.C. or standing on Evita's balcony in Buenos Aires. JayJay, standing next to me, asked if I were afraid and before I could answer she wrestled the gun away from him and shot him in the head.

"Quite the dream, Covey. Typical white fantasy about the physical superiority of black people."

"I don't know about that. Maybe the Mandingo Myth or the general sense of the well-endowed black male might suggest that."

"Which myth do you want, or need, dispelled?" she asked.

"Neither, just note that the physicality myth is about African American males, not women."

"Oh, I see," she said, "so Aaron or, say, you, could withstand my inherited Zulu warrior DNA strength with one arm and I could not possibly take that gun away?"

"Well, yeah, I think so? What do you say, or should I extend the myth to black women as well?"

"Do what you wish, Chunky White Boy, but FYI, I am a 3rd dan Taekwondo Master."

"So that explains the strong legs. I can hardly wait to dream again."

Chapter 55
Highways and Byways

The Eisenhower Administration did a solid when it greenlit the Inter-State highway system in 1956. It, excuse the pun, paved the way for NAFTA, and it allowed JayJay and me to get to McKinney by I-20 to I-30 just before Ft. Worth onto the LBJ Freeway in Dallas (think the D.C. Beltway with three times the pick-ups) then connect with I-75 north to McKinney. What travelers lost on the interstates were many small towns and marvelous hole in the wall restaurants, the avoidance of which probably added years of life to some folks, but they also gained travel time. The whole trip was now less than eight hours. I never drive Texas roads without thinking of a postcard I once saw as a child (I was appalled at the grammar, but I have grown up since):

> The sun has riz;
> The sun has set;
> And here we is;
> In Texas yet.

JayJay and I were following up a tip from Darwin's beautiful friend, Donnie Peters (hush!). Not only had Aaron's car been in place the whole two weeks, it seemingly had never moved. Donnie had seen a pretty blonde coming or going on a couple of occasions, but there had been no sign of Aaron. M.A. had not looked for him with her pseudonyms, but never mind we wanted to see for ourselves what we could see. Perhaps after exploring McKinney, we would pop up to Sherman to visit Austin College to see Dr. Street. Just mentioning his name made me feel like I owed him a brief on *Brown vs. The Board of Education*.

Aaron's house was easy to find. It was just west of 75 on 380 and left on Gerrish Street. The house was no doubt less impressive than his brother's since it was in neither in the booming nouveau riche section southwest of 75 McKinney's nor the old rich section farther east of 75. It was solidly middle class and on the small size. Its neighbors left and right looked like fixer uppers and one had two large Labs roaming inside the front fence. That could not be fun to live with. Aaron's fairly nice wood frame off-white house with a backyard chain-link fence looked like a fading 1950s dream home. His 1992 green Camaro parked on the right side of a more recently constructed exterior two-car garage had a blue "Go 'Boys" football sticker and a tattered "Bush for Governor" decal on the back bumper.

"OK," I said, "time to swing into action."

Chapter 56
No Tell

I love watching JayJay on stage. The acoustics are great at the Globe and she is always mic'ed up, so she can speak in a natural voice. She prefers small, subtle gestures but she can be broad and bombastic if needed. To get into a role she likes to wear a piece of wardrobe or jewelry that helps her with the character. For her Katerina in *Shrew* she tried to get a small tiara as close to Elizabeth Taylor's (in the movie version) as possible both to channel the character and the great actress as well. At Sewell's, she chose Laura Petrie black slacks to pair with her blue company shirt with the Sewell's Toyota logo. Boy, did it work! The 90s nostalgia for the 60s really paid off for her.

Today, however, her role required a sensible brown dress, comfortable brown flats, small diamond earrings, and a thick black notebook in hand. She also bought cheap silver reading glasses, so no one would suspect that she actually had style. The earrings were Freddie's and the Calvin Klein pink thong underneath her disguise was all her. She was now Brenda Thomas, insurance investigator. Her newly minted business card read:

Brenda Thomas
AAAA Insurance Investigations
1-800-555-6969.
All Across Texas

M.A. made up and produced ten business cards but suggested that JayJay just show them rather than hand them out. We thought she looked fit for business and fit for the performance. She took the car to Roberts' Trailer Repair and Service while I nursed a coffee at a new Starbucks on 75. Why the hell is a small coffee called tall? Over time, they will no doubt fix that and almost certainly lower the price- if they want to stay in business. Anyway, we had a new theory about Aaron's whereabouts and the only way to prove it was to make a personal appearance as an insurance fraud investigator. JayJay had studied the business, rehearsed the role, and was ready to go. She herself wanted to avoid being "marked" as a fraud.

It was show time.

Chapter 57
The Investigator

Roberts was a surprisingly large place with both rental trailers and commercial trailers all over the corner lot. There was a small office building in front of a large garage out back. JayJay and I had driven by earlier, so she knew how to approach the building. She had a rental car, so no one could make our private car back at Enterprise.

As she walked in, she saw a young man at the front counter, but she also quickly noted an inner office off the counter to the left. The older guy in it might just be a manager type. He had the white shirt, gray pants, and too-wide blue tie for the job.

"May I help you?" asked the young guy.

Military crisp JayJay replied, "Brenda Thomas, Quadruple A. May I speak with HR?"

"Uh, you wanna talk with Doug Morehouse, our manager?"

"Sure," she said, "we can start there."

"Hey, Doug, this lady wants to see you!" he yelled.

The older guy in the office looked up and JayJay instantly said to the front counter clerk:

"Thanks, I'll just go to him."

She walked over quickly, and he did not exactly object, but one could see that meeting the public was not his favorite thing, or maybe it was this particular member of the public.

JayJay walked right in and showed him her card. He mumbled hello and looked at it quizzically. She took it back with a comment that she had not brought enough cards for this trip.

Doug asked her to sit and really spoke for the first time.

"What's this about? I covered everything with Global two weeks ago."

"Yes, sir, I read the incident report, but we are employed by the company to check things out to be sure the claimant is not milking the insurance."

"Sure, OK, but it was pretty serious," Doug said.

"Yes sir, I know, but can he in any way claim negligence on Roberts' part after the fact?"

"I can't hardly see that. It happened on the customers' lot when he was about to bring one of their short hall trailers over here."

"Yes?" she asked.

"I mean that customer, that kid, well young man, came out of nowhere and plowed into his cab when his brakes failed. He came into that lot way too fast. I know he thought the cab was empty and he was trying to avoid hitting the workers but how's that our fault?"

"No, but we have to be ready should they make representations later. And is Aaron doing his PT?"

"In the hospital yes and he will do so later in town. But a broke leg, several ribs, and that concussion...he's lucky to be alive. And this on top of his brother gettin' killed and all."

JayJay wrapped it up.

"And the young man? Any chance he did it on purpose?"

"No, he was tore up he did it. Been to see Aaron two-three times already."

"Thank you, Doug. I appreciate the time."

"Say, since you're here, when's the check for our cab comin' in?"

"Not my Department. I am only the investigator. And their insurance should really pay anyway. You should hear from Global soon," she assured him.

Now we knew. The *Strangers on the Train* theory, if it was ever possible, now seemed at the very least derailed. Aaron won't come our way anytime soon. Besides, after two days without checking my cell phone messages, I found that I had three urgent ones from Jack. All three were variations of the same plea: "There's new information. Get your ass back here as soon as possible."

Visiting the college and old friends in North Texas would have to wait. We had to get back to West Texas to stop a murder: Ours.

Chapter 58
The Blind Man and the Elephant

How do we know something? We experience it. We read a little bit about it. We hear rumors of it. Unless we are experts and devote years of our life to studying something, we only know the parts of a phenomenon that affect us directly. I had an Austin College professor who would get exasperated when a student would say "How could I know that? It happened before I was born?" His answer was always the same: "Read a book!" But what if the book had not been written yet? Upon returning to Odessa, both Jack and Junior Baker had to explain to this blind man that the elephant was, in fact, larger than he knew. We met at Jencks and Associates within an hour after hitting the streets of Odessa. I was now wise to the importance of using my cell phone, so I had alerted Jack and Junior about thirty minutes in advance of Odessa's city limits and they were already at my office waiting when I pulled up. JayJay and I had tacos to go on the road for dinner, so were anxious to spend the time necessary to hear and to digest the new info.

Jack went first.

"There have always been a lot of William O'Tooles in Boston, Covey. M.A. also tells us there is no way yet to track individual people online without already knowing a lot about them. AOL, she says, is of no help. Erica called the Boston Public Library to look at a 1978 phone directory for William O'Tooles and the lady just laughed at her. She then went to the Ector Library to look at microfiche copies of the *Boston Globe* for that year.

206

We do, of course, have Beth's word that their family lived in South Boston until 1978 and we know that her dad was at least marginally criminal. Basically, if our William O'Toole was there, he did not seem to catch the attention of the major newspaper. But one person other than Whitey Bulger, the reputed head of the Winter Hill Gang, did. It was one of that gang's alleged associates in the Blackfriars' Pub Massacre in 1978. The guy's alias was Fast Frankie, the Charming Hitman. Frankie went missing after the Winter Hill bunch supposedly killed 3-4 suspected informants at a local Pub. The paper says that Frankie was known to use a silencer and that he, when not killing people, loved to hold sway by telling stories. That description caught Erica's attention and so did one other line in the article. It was possible, the paper said, that Frankie had gone south for the winter, maybe as far as Texas."

"OK," I said, "it's a bit tangential, but I see the connection you are making. Still, it is circumstantial, no?"

"Absolutely, Covey, but as the TV ads go, 'wait, there's more!' Junior, you take it from here."

"Covey, you are aware of the drug cartels bringing in cocaine, heroin, and Meth to the US, right?"

"Oh, sure," I said, "The Colombians, Pablo Escobar, the Cali Cartel, and all that. Scary folks."

"That's right," Junior said, "but that is old news, I am afraid. I have friends in the FBI and the DEA who tell me there's a new game in town. It looks like Mexican cartels are pushing the Colombians out or they may be carving up the global drug territory between them. It looks increasingly likely that Mexican gangs are already bigger and more powerful than Colombian gangs in the U.S. They are taking advantage of the 2,000-mile border with the U.S. and the new openness of the NAFTA border crossings."

"Hmmm, OK," I replied, "and?"

"And," Junior went on, "one Mexican character call El Chapo is taking particular advantage of semi-barren areas in New Mexico on that long border to bring in drugs and women. And he is directing all this from a Mexican jail cell where he is treated like a privileged guest."

"Let me guess. Does a little town only 30 miles north of Mexico that seems isolated and desolate play a part in this drama?"

Junior replied, "You got it. Deming, New Mexico."

"So," I said with sudden realization, "the Feds are looking into one Wild Bill O'Toole, aka fast Frankie, as a player in assisting Mexican cartels in moving women and drugs into the U.S. through Deming and southwest New Mexico?"

"That would be a yes," Junior said. "The cartels need help on the ground from locals in the U.S."

JayJay weighed in, "Why would Bill go on a killing spree now? Especially for folks involved in a 1979 crime?"

"The two best reasons I can think of," said Junior, "are that Bill might worry that an old crime could draw law enforcement's attention to him and, if that happened, the Mexicans might look elsewhere other than him for local help."

"But more murders bring more attention," JayJay said.

Junior then hit on it. "Look, criminals are not always that smart, Ms. Qualls. They think they can get away *with* it or get away *from* it. Bill actually has his whole life. Killing a few people now might buy him time and he really doesn't have that many years left. My guess is that this is his biggest score and he wants to ride it off to the sunset."

"But that would mean killing me," JayJay said almost crestfallen. I agreed with her that in a way that would be another father-figure failing another child even if they were in no way related. But perhaps Bill had to kill. He might not really have had an alternative.

Chapter 59
The Minute Freddie Died, March 22, 1979

As talkative as he had been before Freddie got in his car, Bill shut down once they drove away from Freddie's small house. Freddie thought of trying to seduce him, but then as she looked at his anxious face in the moonlight, she thought better of it. Perhaps the right course was to figure out what to do as the night progressed. One good sign was that O'Toole had not been drinking. Men give themselves all kinds of permission when drinking. Within minutes they were approaching the I-20 underpass. The barn was blocks away. This was not a good sign.

The Carletons' Big Red was parked there and the idiot brothers were out of it waiting. The young one had something in his right hand. A gun? No, a knife.

"Bill, you takin' me up in here to get hurt?"

"No, Sugar, no. They just wanna talk. I'll tell Aaron to put that damn frog sticker away. We just need your help."

They parked, left the lights on, and approached. Delbert pulled open the barn door. The Carletons had lied to Bill. In fact, they suspected Bill had ratted them out. Unlike him, they had been drinking.

"Come inside. I found a lantern I suppose that colored John Wayne hid. We kin talk inside," Delbert said.

"Nah, I ain't goin' in there. You wanna talk, talk here," Freddie insisted.

Aaron chimed in, "Listen, who's got the knife and who's standing in the cold near naked?"

"Then use that fuckin' knife, Pecker Brain," said Freddie. "I ain't goin' in there, period."

Bill tried diplomacy.

"Now come on everyone, calm down. Boys, you said you just wanted to talk."

"To quote the big nigger, shut the fuck up, you Irish Mick," said Delbert, Jr. "We know you was in on this deal. You're probably the reason we got jumped. You and your black-ass girlfriend."

"You chicken shits," Bill exploded. "You lied to me. You said you'd just scare her. Why did I set this raid up? What would I gain?"

"$10,000 or more down the road. You two take away our idea and do the parties without us," Delbert, Jr. said.

"Damn, boy, you supposed to be the smart one," said Bill. "How we gonna take over for you? I work with you now and I did the whole El Paso gig. You boys and I are just partners and you got the Legion contacts."

"Yeah," said Aaron, "but your nigger friend here got the muscle to steal the girls and crash our little barn dance. How did they know?"

Bill turned to Freddie. "Tell 'em, Sug, how did you know? How did that big boy know?"

Freddie was cold but at least they were talking. Maybe they would keep talking.

"You give yourselves away. That's how we knew. One of our associates saw you in Juarez talkin' to girls and we found out," said Freddie.

"That don't matter now," said Delbert. "I don't believe it but it don't matter. We want them girls back

211

tonight or we lose $10,000. The shit hit the fan when we went to the hotel. Them men want their money back and we already spent half of it. Get them girls back or we take $10,000 out of your hide."

"I ain't got no $10,000 and the girls are on the way back to El Paso," said Freddie.

What happened next was a blur. Delbert, Jr. grabbed Freddie's arm to drag her into the barn. Bill pushed Delbert away with both hands. Aaron clubbed Bill in the back of the head with the blunt end of the knife. Freddie, a strong woman, rushed Aaron to help Bill but he turned and plunged the knife deep into her chest. She died instantly.

"You stupid shits," Bill screamed. "We needed her girls for the party. If we had to, we hold her hostage or use her as leverage somehow. You stupid, unprofessional, idiots. You only kill if you have to!"

The three white men stood in shock. Nobody was supposed to die that night. Bill was woozy and furious. Delbert, Jr. could not believe his eyes. Aaron hardly knew what he had done. Idiots though they were, they knew they had to get away fast. The three of them picked up her body and placed it in the ditch next to the access road to the barn just to get it farther away from their property. Delbert, Jr. used the lantern to locate car tracks, perhaps to somehow brush them away, but from the last two days there had been so much traffic, he decided that the cops would not learn anything from the tracks anyway. He forgot the knife. They really made multiple mistakes, but in the end there was no real investigation and the Odessa police did even talk to them about a body found near their property. But the brothers knew they had to leave Odessa. They knew their lives would never be the same. $10,000 was the cost of their ruined futures.

Freddie lay dead on Old Crane Highway next to a decrepit barn.

Chapter 60
Only in West Texas

November 1996 brought new shocks to what we thought we knew about West Texas. That month Ector County elected a Democrat as Sheriff. Not only that, it turned out that Democrat was a black man. Reggie Yearwood was his name. The respective roles of sheriffs and police chiefs always confused me, though I knew sheriffs are elected and chiefs are appointed (by the city council). Both are law enforcement and in Texas, their duties and jurisdictions often overlap. When it came to the cartels and drugs in the U.S. southwest, the DEA, FBI, etc. coordinated with either the Odessa Police Department or the Sheriff's Department as need be. Thus, I chose to go to the Sheriff's Office, at long last, to detail my suspicions about the connections between murders in 1979 and 1996 and another expected attempted murder in late 1996 or early 1997. It took a while to cover it all, but my story was not dismissed out of hand. I also had the feeling that giving them O'Toole's name confirmed something, or someone, for them. However, at the end of the meeting, I was not altogether relieved.

"Mr. Jencks, thank you for your information. It may be of potential use to us," said the Deputy.

"Does it give you enough to arrest O'Toole?"

"We couldn't even if we wanted to since the incident of Delbert Carleton's death occurred in Frisco, TX and O'Toole lives in NM, but I will share notes with my colleagues both at the state and Federal levels."

214

"Can you protect us, uh, my friend and me?" I asked.

"We do not have the resources to do that and the story, while interesting, requires confirmation through investigation, something that we simply can't undertake at this time. If you are worried, maybe going back to D.C. might be your best option."

Chapter 61
Playing Telephone

JayJay sighed and said, "So *Strangers on a Train* seems unlikely. Do we now switch to *Usual Suspects*"?

I responded, "Yeah, and now it seems that Wild Bill is Keyser Soze."

Truth be told I did not feel like I completely knew what I was doing but I did know what to do next: provoke a killer. We actually had ruled no one out yet, well maybe except Delbert, but of those left, Bill seemed like the most likely suspect to have murdered someone lately. Aaron was convalescing in a hospital; Dan and Bo Gladstone were lying low; and Bill's past was putting him in better present focus. Bill would seem to have the greatest incentive to take action. Part of me worried that in trying to solve Freddie's murder I had gotten Delbert killed, but given the clear and present danger to JayJay and me, I could not fret over that. What I had to do now was create a scenario where the killer had to worry what JayJay and I would do next so that he, or they, would do something that the Odessa Sheriff's department would have to stop. Gulp!

"I told Wild Bill that if I ever decided to tell the police about his involvement, I would call him," I told JayJay. "Now's the time."

"I guess I agree," she replied. "He may already have done something to Delbert, but anyway, waiting for something to happen to us would be worse than just getting it over."

"I want to keep you out of it," I said.

"You know that's impossible. I know what you know, and he knows that I know. He won't be sentimental, and you can't be either," she asserted.

"But I am."

"Get over it. But let's do this right!"

Again, it took several calls to reach Bill. That alone made me nervous. Was he on the move? Was he out coordinating drug trafficking? Or was he at the Silver Bucket telling exaggerated stories? Finally, he answered.

"Bill, this is Covey Jencks."

"Mr. Jencks. How are you and how's my girl? What can I do you for?"

"We are both fine. Just got back from a quick trip to North Texas. I hope you are well, Mr. O'Toole."

"Sure, sure, all good here except for a bit of arthritis. North Texas, eh? Missing big city life?"

Wow, he is good, I was thinking. All small talk and not any sense of urgency or alarm. I, on the other hand, felt shaky and hopeful that I could deliver the message that I had to deliver.

"Dallas?" I said, "No, we didn't go to Dallas, just through it on the way to Sherman where I went to college, Austin College. Dropped by to see an old professor friend."

"Very thoughtful of you. And now you remember ole Bill way out here in the New Mexican desert?"

"Yes, well, you know I came to a decision that I promised to tell you about."

"You and Bonnie Jay are tying the knot? That is wonderful."

(OK, now that is really good. Pretend you don't recall. Very good.)

"No, Bill, not yet, but that is another call I will make when it's time. It's on that other matter."

"Oh, it's about your conscience, right?"

"Yes, Delbert's dead. I figure Aaron did it to shut him up. And now he might want to come after, you know, either you or me, maybe JayJay. I think I need to tell the cops what I know about what happened in 1979."

"You're worried about idiot Aaron?"

(Did you just reveal that you know something, Wild Bill?)

"Yeah, sure, I mean we know he has killed before." Pause. "Though, of course, he is not a professional or anything."

"My thoughts exactly," said Bill.

"Anyway, JayJay and I have come to a decision to let the cops know to see if we can get some protection or something."

"OK, that's unlikely, but I see what you mean. This implies that my role in the 1979 event has to be part of your chat with the Sheriff's Office?"

"Yeah, I am afraid it has to be. So, I thought I'd warn you."

"When is this happening?"

"Next Monday morning at 9:00 AM."

"So," Bill concluded, "In five days? All wrapped up before Christmas?"

"Yeah, just wanted you to know and hope you understand."

218

"Certainly, me boy, I do. A man's gotta do what a man's gotta do. We all do."

"Thanks, Bill, take care."

"I will, Covey, I will. Oh, and, say Covey, if Aaron might really be after you, I'd leave that house on Santa Rita and move somewhere else temporarily, say a motel or something on the other side of town."

He hung up.

"Oh, shit," I said.

"What?" JayJay said.

"He knows where we are."

"We don't have to wonder how" was her reply.

"No, it's either Dan Gladstone or Bo, or both, informing him," I said.

"My money is on Dan," she said.

Chapter 62
Odessa 1975 Bonham Junior High

Junior High was hard enough without having to worry about Bo Gladstone every day. While I played football and baseball and served on the Student Council, I was still best known for making good grades.

Well, perhaps, it was not just making good grades, but caring about good grades that got me in trouble. Somehow, we were not supposed to care, especially if we were real men. I cared. I cared so much that I actually volunteered when our speech teacher, Miss White, asked the class to simulate a debate. My debate opponent was to be Bo Gladstone. The topic was pro or con on the proposition that "Desegregation is a good thing."

I am not sure if Miss White wanted to stir something up or not, but I was asked to argue the affirmative and Bo was asked to assume the negative. Bo seemed offended that he was asked, offended by the topic, and offended by his opponent. When he took the lectern, he simply said, "I am against it." Miss White asked why, and Bo looked at her like she was the dumbest person on the planet and said, "Busing."

Miss White asked if he could elaborate and Bo said, "This is stupid" and sat down. Miss White indicated that it was my turn. I went behind the lectern and said, "So if this were a real debate, I guess I'd win if I could simply articulate a full sentence." The class laughed, but Bo came out of his seat like a shot. He would have hit me too if he hadn't tripped on someone's backpack. The class laughed again, and I said, "Sorry, Bo, I just meant to clarify the rules. No offense."

But offense was taken. Later he told me that if I ever showed him up again, I'd be a dead man. I believed him, too. I saw how violent his brother was when I found him beating up Bo with a strap when we were in the 7th grade. Later, 8th grade I think, I saw Dan and Bo beat up a couple of fairly big Hispanic guys when they dared to show up at "our" Youth Club dance. They were just outside the door of the Y and the fight was so vicious kids didn't even watch. They got the hell out of there. I did as well. Those two incidents and once in a football practice when Bo elbowed me in the head not once but maybe five times were enough to teach me that Bo Gladstone was a vicious bully just like his older brother. I tried to stay away from him the rest of the way through high school. It was another reason I was glad to quit football my senior year. Coaches, by the way, loved Bo. He had fire in his belly.

Now Bo and Dan were back in my life and I had to assume the affirmative that they meant to settle a score with me.

Chapter 63
All Hands, on Deck

"It must be what happened after Freddie died," I said. "Dan might have been paid off to ignore what the Carletons were doing at the parties and maybe to let them off for killing Freddie, but there has to be more," I said.

JayJay responded, "You think the Gladstones have been involved with Bill and the Mexicans?"

"Maybe or maybe they just reconnected with Bill once we started snooping around. They have plenty to cover up and a pension to protect," I said.

"That pension can't be worth that much," she said. "There has to be more."

"Well, maybe. Maybe Bill never did retire and he and the Gladstones have been helping the highest bidder get drugs and girls into the U.S. ever since" I said.

"Where do they live?"

"Huh?" I asked cleverly.

JayJay said, "Well, do they live in houses, drive cars, or take fancy foreign trips beyond their means? If so, we need to know."

"Right!" I said. "I will ask Jack and M.A. to check on it on it. And, by the way, where do *we* go live now?" Pause "We don't check out of the Suites," I added. "I figure the funnyman front desk clerk reports to Dan. We head to your place on the south side and we put Willie back on retainer."

"Good, she said." "I think Willie might need to recruit a few others as well."

"Good idea. As I always say, we can use all the help we can get."

Chapter 64
Now It's Personal

"Covey, this is Jack," he said as I answered my cell.

"Hey! 'Lil. Jack, what you got for me?"

"You were right," he said.

"OK, that's once," I said. "About what?"

"You know, I told you I saw the Gladstone boys in Brownwood back a few years," he said.

Brownwood Texas is about 200 miles from Odessa and it has a beautiful fish-filled lake.

"Yep," I said.

"This morning M.A. checked with real estate sales in Brown County records. Her sister's cousin is the Records Clerk there. Ain't Texas somethin'? Dan Gladstone bought a beautiful lakeside home on Lake Brownwood in '87. I figured out that it's the one with a huge boat docked there up there on Mountainview Lane. I'd assume that it's beyond their means on his salary and I bet they paid cash before such purchases were so heavily scrutinized. Shall I check more?"

"No need, Jack. That's valuable info and all I need for now. Thanks."

"Cove, I want to do more."

"Really, why Jack? You were the one wanting to keep the firm out of it."

He said, "I know but with the Gladstones, it's personal. And bringing drugs into the US? That's downright unpatriotic. That shit ruins lives. I consider stopping them my duty."

"You are a very fine man, Jack. You are full time now. At least for the three days, we think we have left."

Chapter 65
Covey's Plan

I have always been a planner. In part I saw my dad always planning his next business steps, so that influenced me. But, in truth, something in my DNA compelled me to plan. Getting into shape for football took two years and many different steps from diet to exercise to mental preparation. That started it with me. Plan everything in step-by-step logical sequences. So, making the grades necessary to get a college scholarship, going to law school, getting military experience, securing a clerkship, and going to D.C. entered my mind as "Life's Plan" when I was barely 16.

Granted I expected to stay in D.C. longer than nine months, but the plan worked. My plan to build Jencks and Associates based on how my dad did business also worked, though I admit luck played a bigger role. The most important plan was how to solve the Freddie case and that also worked though not quite like I dreamed it. The point is to have in mind an end goal, to have certain crucial steps mapped out to reach that goal, and to make sure that all the resources are in place to make things happen. Right now, I had to plan how to stop two murders for which I had an approximate date and by whom I had probable suspects using resources that I liked but might not be sufficient. Sounded tentative to me, but time was of the essence.

Chapter 66
Wild Bill's Plan

Bill chuckled to himself when he thought about the lawyer. Probably thought of himself as some kind of detective or something. Funny that he would call indicating that he would talk to the cops in five days. He has almost certainly already told the cops and probably even told them suspicions of my past and possible current crimes. He has no idea! Thinks he does but has no idea.

How could anyone suspect that Bill had been working on this get rich and famous scheme for twenty years now and that more than a handful of small-town officials were already in his pocket? Gladstone, the Odessa cop, was the first to turn and maybe the easiest, but from California to Central Texas, he could call in chips from friends for help if he wanted. But he didn't want to. Slightly mentally unhinged but still clever, he liked the thrill of being "the guy" again, just like Boston. He didn't need to sully his hands on this kid, but then he wanted to. The punk and his dad had it coming back then but Bill had to lay low for a long time after Freddie died. When he was ready to deal with Frank, the old guy came down with throat cancer. Better to let him suffer with that than let him off the hook by killing him quickly. That was Wild Bill's specialty, the quick kill. Karma though brought his son back, so now the kid could get his. That will settle the score. Fucking Frank setting up Freddie to bust his operation and take it over. If Aaron hadn't killed her, Bill would have had to. There's no room for sentiment in this business. The thing about Bill was his patience. The fucking Texas amateurs just had no idea.

This would be sweet. Covey and that nigger gal will think he will hit them before Monday. Fat chance! They would be ready. Monday night might work but it'd be best to hit them early Wednesday morning, say around midnight or 1:00 AM. They might try to leave their room at the Suites, but it really doesn't matter where they go. Once they make a move, Bradley, the front desk clerk, will track them. It's hilarious he left Odessa while they were at the Suites, rammed Aaron Carleton, and got back before Covey and the nigger gal missed him. He even visited Aaron a couple of times so when he goes back to kill him, he will know the layout of the hospital. He is a good young partner, like me at that age, and he was easy to recruit when Covey lived there last year. A handful of cash can buy a lot of help.

Everybody has let him down his whole life. Whitey, Frank, his hateful wife, Freddie, and the big shot Colombians. Now the Mexicans. Sure, they let him run some girls and some weed, but they just use his barn in Deming as a temporary storage place. It's easy money but they never let him take product farther downstream. So, he didn't speak Spanish? So, what? Things may be changing now with El Chapo. He's the real deal, though he's pretty crazy to kill people at times. Then there's Dan Gladstone. He always pushes for more action and more pay. Damn Texans, no patience. Too reckless.

Come next Wednesday I settle a debt, head to Mexico for a while, and later get back in with a new name and new place. My biggest score ever. Lived OK for twenty years but coming soon, I will be a boss. Fucking Whitey and the gang. Who needs ya?

Chapter 67
JayJay's Plan

Freddie said it best. "Men always leave." They die. They take off for younger women. They get run out of town. They turn to drink. Best to stay away, keep uninvolved. Black or white, it doesn't matter. At an early age, I made a pledge to myself: Never again will I get married. Never again will I depend on a man.

So, how did this happen? How did I end up not only loving this guy but trusting his judgment about life and death? All my instincts say to be cautious, protect myself, but all my thoughts turn to how to protect *us* against killers and racists. "The course of true love never did run smooth," Shakespeare said. If we die, maybe our story will inspire a play or at least a country and western song. What a silly thought.

Stop thinking that way and think! What have we missed? Chaos is what we have missed. The best-laid plans and all that. Why am I thinking in literature and poems? Covey is the logical one and I am the literary one. Maybe that's why? Why am I so worried? It's the chaos in the universe. That's why. Every step of the way, something unexpected or unimagined has happened. Why not in the end game? How can we prepare for chaos? How can we not? I am in this heart and soul but it's better to live a difficult life than to die a romantic death. The Bard also said: "I will follow thee to the last gasp with truth and loyalty." Covey Jencks, you have my loyalty but you are also gettin' my truth!

Chapter 68
Dan Gladstone's Plan

What is it now? Sixteen-seventeen years? What a long time without a real payoff? Things were going the right way for so long until Covey Jencks came back to Odessa. I remember him as a kid. Always the smart one. Always thinking he was better than everyone. Just because he had a rich daddy and that pretty girlfriend, Callie. He rubbed it in everyone's faces. Look at what he did to Bo. Always making him look bad, always getting him in trouble. That time in junior high when Covey made fun of Bo and Bo took after him. Never even touched him, but he had to go into the Vice Principal's office for five licks. Welts on his ass for a week and a warning to leave Jencks alone or else. In football, Bo was a starter, played his heart out. And what did we hear? Man, did you see Covey on the kick-offs! Another tackle inside the twenty-yard line! Like he was alone out there? Covey got those tackles because the rest of the team closed off lanes and pushed the backs up the middle. That was how it was supposed to work. It's a team game after all. That's the Permian Panthers' way.

I never played football. I had to work before and after school because our sorry ass dad was too drunk to hold a job, but I made sure Bo got to play and he was good. Full scholarship to Central Oklahoma. He just didn't have the smarts to make it through. Once he got hurt, where were the tutors to help him them? Damn university, they didn't care. They were done with him. I have been taking care of Bo all his life and the only teams I have been on have been the army and the police. Now this thing with Bill. Wrap things up and everything changes. I think we have all the lanes blocked so the has only one way to go. Then it will be over and see who comes out on top this time. A long wait is almost over.

Chapter 69
Chaos in the Universe

West Texas is largely defined by two products of nature, or natural processes anyway. One is the decaying of things, like dinosaurs, over the millennia. That decay gave rise to the presence of oil. Oil became the foundation of energy in the world and energy became the driving force of commerce and politics globally. Eventually, the oil under the ground will be tapped out. It will be gone. It won't happen at the same places at the same time, but it will happen. Oh, technology will extend its presence for decades to come, but it is a finite resource and West Texans, even today, know what's coming. That is why windmills now dot the Texas landscape and why city planners constantly debate how to diversify the economy. It hasn't happened yet, but they keep planning. Tourism is probably not the long-term answer but with museums, meteor craters, and music festivals, West Texans keep trying. One thing that holds West Texas back and will seemingly forever be a problem is the severe impact of another fact of nature that defines West Texas as much as the presence of oil. That is the process that often generates the absence of water. Water sustains life. Its absence renders life impossible.

Periodically weather patterns in the Pacific Ocean create cooler surface temperatures which ironically create warmer, drier conditions in the Southwest of the U.S. This is called La Nina and the opposite condition, El Nino, results in cooler, wetter conditions. These alternating phenomena have also existed for time immemorial.

233

Tectonic plates may dictate the contours of the land, but weather mostly determines what grows and dies upon it. Floods and droughts are but natural processes. The worst periods for drought and warm weather in West Texas in the twentieth century were the 1930s and the 1950s. The conditions of the latter period persisted for eight years. Crops like cotton were ruined. Livestock numbers dwindled in size and died of thirst. Water rationing was necessary; green lawns turned brown; and the wind blew. These conditions began in Mexico and spread to West Texas and New Mexico. Call them another Mexican import that Texans didn't want but were seemingly helpless to control. As luck and the universe would have it, after the 50s the next big drought for West Texas was in 1995/96. It was just in time to affect the end game that I had initiated nearly three years earlier when I came back to Odessa.

The wind blew.

Chapter 70
Come the Day

December 10, 1996

Bill's plan was to leave on the Tuesday after Covey's meeting was supposed to have occurred. He allowed nine hours for the trip, so he'd eat lunch at the Bucket before noon and then hit the road. The green 1995 Chevy van was loaded. The only piece of equipment he really needed was his new 9 mm Glock with the 30 mm suppressor (silencer), a state-of-the-art weapon with the silencer sights lining up perfectly with the Glock sights. Bill bought it and its hard-plastic case at a Gun Show in Albuquerque. He used a false identity and paid cash. He passed a quick background check because he had paid for false documents under the name James R. Ray of Albuquerque. The Glock sat right next to his two large suitcases filled with all the clothes he would need for this trip. All he had to do was hook up with I-10, head southeast through El Paso, link to I-20 heading northeast just outside of Pecos, and scoot on in to Odessa. It was a long trip, but, as long as he stayed awake on the monotonous road, it was an easy one.

Everything and everyone was in place in Odessa. He doubled checked it all just before he left the house. At 72 Bill did not have a cell phone and he did not intend to buy one. He had already heard that the FBI was now using something called the Sting Ray to track suspects. Not him, not Bill. He was proud to be a step ahead on that one. Phone calls they could trace back to him later in Deming, but that's OK. He would not be there. He had been there much longer than he ever intended anyway. The weather was gorgeous today. It was 67 degrees, winds at 17 miles per hour, and very low humidity.

Dan appreciated Bill's phone call before he set off for work. It was Go Day, though the real action would occur at night, actually early Wednesday morning. If everything went smoothly, it would be a new world later Wednesday morning. If he survived…things could go wrong in combat. He knew that from Nam and from other dust-ups with the OPD. He was no Rex Young hero, but he had been in firefights and shootouts. It's not at all like the movies and the biggest challenge is managing the fear and keeping your wits. Just come out the other end. The good thing is that his side had the element of surprise. That was the best thing. Debts would be settled, and surprises awaited. Two good things.

Covey and JayJay were feeling nervous. Seventy-two hours ago, they stayed up all night talking about JayJay's concerns about assumptions and chaos. Covey got brownie points for listening but then he already felt a bit on shaky ground with his own estimates and considerations, so he was open to suggestions. The talk prompted a call to the Odessa Police Department which in turn led to a shocking and mildly unsettling revelation. But then it is better to know than not to know, right? The local task force was not altogether happy with Covey's personal heroics, but the absolute truth was that he (and JayJay) bore most of the risk and they had forced a move that could bring some resolution

236

to a long-standing operation, an operation that for the Love Birds carried a major caveat. Unless it went perfectly, one or both of them could die. Oh, and the other thing they discussed was their love for each other. It got awfully sappy, so JayJay ended it in a fairly pointed way. Covey understood the point. They were hoping that would not be the last such, uh, talk they had.

Chapter 71
The Best Laid Plans

Bill had acquired some aspects of Southwestern acculturation after nearly twenty years in Texas and New Mexico. He now listened to classic Country and Western music. Fortunately, he could pick up 103.3, KTBL The Bull, out of Albuquerque, so he set the speed control on 70 and headed east. He would not veer south for nearly 90 miles and the I-10 would dip toward El Paso. Smooth sailing.

Just after Bill hit Las Cruses and turned south, the sky on his right side darkened. At first, he took the creeping darkness as a thundercloud, a quick desert shower that looked menacing but would briefly dissipate as quickly as it gathered. It was not rain, however. The few cars ahead of him were pulling off the highway ahead, so Bill decided to do so as well. He pulled onto the shoulder, glanced to his right, and then he saw it. Coming at him was a 500-foot wall of dust and sand that must have been five miles wide.

He could not run, and he could not hide. He had either to get back in the van, stay put, and hunker down no matter how long it took, or he needed to drive on through slowly and hope he was not blown off course or hit by debris, or worse, another vehicle. Going slowly forward was not the safest bet but it was the one he chose. He felt he had to. The operation depended on him. He hurriedly jumped back into the van and drove three minutes before the 40 mile an hour wind hit him with a sandblast that rocked the vehicle and blew him partially into the lane coming the opposite direction.

Covey and JayJay did not let down their guard when nothing happened on Monday, so it was no big surprise when the call came in on Tuesday morning. It was Willie on his cell.

"He is on the move and he just pulled on to I-10 traveling east. I will follow at a safe distance and let you know if he is Odessa-bound."

"Thanks, Willie, stay invisible, OK?"

"Roger that."

JayJay had insisted that Bill be monitored and followed; Willie was the man for the job. Willie wanted to "stop" Bill, but both Covey and JayJay thought that was way too risky. There might come a time but not yet. When the storm hit, Willie had to move closer to Bill and when he pulled off I-10 for a second time, Willie pulled past and drove for twenty more minutes at 30 MPH before he reached daylight and found a clear spot to park on a farm-to-market road from where he'd see Bill as he passed through the sandstorm to safety. Willie knew that Bill would now be behind schedule and he'd need at least a couple of stops before getting to Odessa. He tried to call Covey to alert him, but he could not get a signal out on the lonely desert.

Dan wasn't sure of the timing for the day, but he had his orders. If it all went right, it would be quick. The big complication for Dan was lack of sleep. He had spent Monday night at Bo's house talking into the wee hours about the problems his brother had with State Farm. Bo may or may not have over-charged a large number of people for

239

home insurance and he may or may not have suggested that some folks had coverage that the insurance documents proved he had not, in fact, sold them. Few homes had flood insurance in West Texas and few needed it but two springs ago two homes near the golf course had flooded and based on what Bo had told them, the owners expected payment. Dan did not get to bed until after midnight and then Bo's 11-month-old twins serenaded the household with screams and cries for two more hours. But on Tuesday, the big day, Go Day, he was downtown by 7:00 AM. It had to be just a normal day. At 10:00 AM Bill called Dan's dedicated cell. It's a Go.

Chapter 72
Zero Hour

Sandstorms range from mini dust devils that swirl and kick up sand for less than a minute to what Bill encountered, a massive tidal wave of sand that covered miles of ground and advanced on its target area steadily over the course of thirty minutes to an hour. Trapped inside a car a person can literally feel the grains of sand penetrate the vehicle and cover one's clothes, car interior, and any exposed valuables. Visibility, which is normally to the far horizon, can shrink to a mile and feel like just a few feet. The wind buffets the car and its roar even drowns out thought. Bill had been in a sandstorm but never one out on the road. He was not sure if another storm lay ahead or if this one event was it, but was it an omen of things going wrong all day long? All he knew is that he had lost time; he needed a shower; and he worried if any dust had gotten into his Glock. It seemed to be everywhere else. Nevertheless, in an instant, it suddenly stopped and then he could see a few other vehicles ahead and behind him. He would press on but now every other thought was "What a God-forsaken place this is!"

Willie picked up Bill what turned out to be just a few miles before the loop around El Paso. That loop and the El Paso skyline made him nostalgic for the days and nights he had spent in Juarez. Nothing tempted him to go back now, but memories of the Swank Club, China, and the old days floated through his head. Curiously Bill was part of the reason he had never been back and he disliked the old bastard even more for that. He tried calling Covey again, but still, there was no signal.

JayJay and Covey knew that something was going down on Tuesday night. They had moved back into the Suites. They ate a late dinner at Ben's Little Mexico now located on Grand Avenue, but the food was every bit as good as it had always been. Covey's mantra all day was "trust the plan," though JayJay literally cringed every time she heard it, in part because their role was so passive for the big showdown.

The Task Force was mobilized. They had professionals. Federal, State and local law enforcement were all involved. The Love Birds, the Task Force called them, knew that minutes after Bill left the Deming city limits New Mexican authorities, using the RICO Act provisions and a warrant, entered Bill's house in Deming and immediately began searching for evidence on Bill's connections to the Mexicans and for directions to properties or storage areas nearby that the gangs used prior to wider distribution of the narcotics. It was not as good as hitting the gang in Mexico itself, but it was time to disrupt this particular entry point. In Odessa, every step JayJay and Covey took was mapped, covered, and, one hoped, protected. After dinner, they returned to the Suites and parked the Camry in the same spot as they usually did. They walked up the same outside stairs. And they even nodded and said hello to another couple as they approached from the opposite side of the building to their room next to JayJay's and Covey's. Sleep was not the order of the evening, but the plan called for lights out at 11:00 PM, just thirty minutes away.

A little past the cut-off to Pecos, Willie got through.

"Covey, he has stopped at a Love's Truck Stop for dinner. I will grab a burger ahead and pick him up down the road. You good?"

"We are good, Willie. How you holding up?" I asked.

"It's all good. Ran into a sandstorm, but came out the other side, just as we all will tonight. I will call when he hits the Odessa city limits," he said.

I felt professional when I replied, "Roger that, Willie."

He did call at 11:30 PM. "He is in Odessa, but he's pulled into a motel. I am gonna sit on him a while. I assume that he is showering and resting up."

I had to go to the window to look out onto the parking lot to see if everything was in place. I am not sure if it felt great or terrifying that I could not see a thing. Still, I know that the Task Force must know what Willie knew. Bill was in town. We are talking hours if not minutes before something happens. They were not one bit too happy about Willie's involvement, but frankly, we insisted and we did not even have to say "it's because we need someone we trust involved." The deal was that he always stayed on the perimeter. After all, it was our life on the line. In the end, they agreed.

"And what did you do in the war, daddy?"

"Why, son, your mom and I played gin rummy virtually the whole time."

Under the covers with a flashlight waiting for a phone call. Then it came. At 2:30 AM, Wednesday, December 11.

"He is moving. Just came off 2nd Street where 2nd and 8th merge into old highway 80. Heading toward the Suites, I reckon," said our main man.

"OK, thanks, Willie."

Bill came east on 80, approached the Suites, slowed, and then kept going. He actually for the first time sped up. Did he blink his lights as he went by? Maybe.

Meanwhile, Bradley, the smart ass front desk clerk, stationed in a third-floor Suites' room just above Covey's place, had seen the Chevy Van drive by and blink its lights. He and Bill had figured that when he drove by and didn't stop, the cops would assume that Bill had seen them and called off the hit. They would then relax their guard and maybe even go home. Five minutes went by and then Bradley saw a car at the far north end of the lot pull out. It had worked. They were packing up. Stupid Odessa cops. He waited ten more minutes.

No one had marked him. He worked at the front desk for a year. He had access to keys to every room and he knew well the floorplan of the Love Birds' suite. He even had a steel cutter if they locked the chain on their door. They really should invest in better dead-bolt locks at this cheap place. An inside job. No one saw that coming. Just as he had walked into the Methodist Hospital in McKinney early this morning and killed Aaron Carleton, this hit would be simple. Open the door, shoot the idiots, get out of town, and join Bill in Mexico. Then there would be no more witnesses to the old man's crimes, he'd be $100,000 richer, and they'd both have a new life. What will the papers call him? Bradley the Kid? He liked that.

Glock in hand he slipped out his door. Slowly and quietly he went down the outer hall and descended the stairs. He approached the room that Covey and JayJay had called home for two weeks this time around. No one confronted him. No one yelled at him. No one maybe even saw him. He placed the key in the handle and it opened easily. There was no chain. He simply had to open the door wider to see the two figures lying in the king size in the dark. Ah, the Love Birds, they were separated only by a few inches. He fired multiple shots into each body.

At the same time, Bill was speeding towards Midland having pulled off of Business 80 back onto to I-20. Call him the long-run decoy or call him the criminal mastermind, he was thinking. He had learned a lot from Whitey Bulger in Boston. Not everything is done with muscle. Some of it has to be done with cunning and deception. He knew how to tell a story. Convince a naïve young man that you are a big-time gangster, offer him money to do your bidding, and then leave him high and dry. Work a corrupt cop for years and assure him that there'd be a big pay off and then, just when there were real opportunities, disappear. When did Dan Gladstone show-up, he tried to remember? Right before the Golden Hotel and the plan to bring in Mexican girls? He was too eager to help then and he's too eager now. Did Bill tell him too much over the years about the marijuana or about the girls? Maybe. But nothing ever came of it. Odessa was a steady market, but Gladstone every few years pushed him to expand the operation and to connect him to his Colombian and now Mexican contacts. Too impatient. Too eager. Too stupid, but marginally useful nevertheless. He did play a small role in telling Bill when that Do-Gooder Covey Jencks showed up. Snooping around in an accidental death from 1979 and stumbling into Bill's business! How in the world did he show up exactly at the wrong time? Chaos in the universe! Good to be rid of both the lawyer and the cop.

Two miles east of Midland Bill saw a highway patrol roadblock ahead. Three cars astride Highway 20 and two more on the access road. He looked in his rearview and sure enough, there was another police vehicle speeding up behind him with lights flashing. Bill realized that he was not just about to get a speeding ticket. He slowed down to accept the inevitability of capture. No hero he.

Willie had stayed well behind Bill, but he had to speed up when Bill accelerated past the 75 MPH speed limit on I-20. Willie was going 80. At first, he thought the approaching cop car with lights flashing would pull him over, so he slowed down. But it didn't stop Willie. It kept going and that's when Willie saw that it was an unmarked cop car, the kind that put the bubble gum machine on top of the car only when needed. Clearly, it was after Bill and not him. Must be the task force at work. Then Willie stopped, crossed over to I-20 west and called Covey. Again, no answer.

Seconds after Bradley fired into the bodies of two dummies arranged in the bed, Dan Gladstone came from behind the hotel door to stick his .45 into Bradley's ribs.

Drop the gun, punk!" Dan said. Bradley did as demanded. At that point, Linda Brown, a black woman who looked just a bit like JayJay, came out of the bathroom with handcuffs drawn. She cuffed Bradley, read him his Miranda

246

rights, and then sat him on the bed without further conversation. Linda then exited the suite and went next door where JayJay and Covey were no doubt wondering what was going on. They had switched rooms with the cop couple earlier in the evening upon returning from dinner and they were still safely behind a temporary, steel-reinforced bar lock on the outer door. Linda knocked twice according to the pre-arranged signal. They were to sit tight.

The backup plan worked. Thanks to JayJay. She loved Covey's logical mind, but she also felt that it was based on too many assumptions about the people involved. Sure, Bill was the obvious player, but the *Usual Suspects* Theory exaggerated Bill's capabilities and brains. The *Strangers on a Train* idea brought Delbert and Aaron into the story in a tenuous way and it depended on Dan Gladstone being a killer cop. To her, Aaron was not smart enough to come up with this scheme and maybe Dan was shady, but a killer? How in the world had he even stayed on the force all these years? Not giving him a promotion was not sufficient punishment if he really was dirty? If the whole Odessa Police Department was not in on it, and she frankly doubted that they were, then maybe there was another explanation. Let's assume that he is playing dirty and is not really corrupt. Where does that take us? It takes us to talking to the police. That led in turn to a revelation and a shock. There was already a Fed, state, and local task force investigating drug trafficking in Texas and New Mexico. Dan was part of it.

We were late to the game. Dan Gladstone long ago had joined the Odessa Police Department Vice Squad. He, years before, had been promoted to detective sans a public announcement. And long ago he started working multiple Texas connections to drug gangs. It meant tolerating some drug activities, supporting a few arrests, and waiting for an inside shot at the heart of the gang activity, though the switch from Colombian to Mexican gangs had caused another long delay. Bill O'Toole was just one of the leads Dan worked on but he was particularly easy to flatter and get talking. The Task Force had been playing the long game with him, but then Covey came along. He forced the action.

JayJay also wanted to assume other persons might play a role. But who? Covey then had an idea. Aaron's accident? Was it really an accident or was it a botched murder? Assume the latter. What did the McKinney Police know about the young customer with the bad brakes? Could they or the hospital provide a description of the guy? Eventually, they could and even though it did not allow them to protect Aaron any better, it did give the Odessa Police Department, with Covey's and JayJay's help, all they needed to identify Bradley Harper, one of the front desk clerks at the Suites' Motel.

The information identifying Bradley as the probable killer came in just late that afternoon after they had found out about Bill's delay with the sandstorm. While they already had the plan to switch rooms, this information alerted them to another danger. Bill might try the hit himself, but then he might just as well leave the killing to the young guy. Plan A was to intercept Bill with the perimeter defense, but Plan B was to use the dummy decoys whoever came in the room to kill Covey and JayJay. If anyone had watched them come into the hotel, they would have had to pay very careful attention that they entered the room next door instead of the one they had been staying in. The Task Force had rented that one, so when Covey and JayJay returned, Linda and Dan just took their room.

Dan knocked on the door to give Covey and JayJay the all clear. It was mildly unsettling for Covey and JayJay now to have to consider him a "good guy." What part of his racist self was real and what was not? In all of this mess, it seemed peculiar to speculate what went "right" with him after all they knew.

"Covey, we have Bradley Harper under arrest. I think we will soon have confirmation that the same is true for William O'Toole."

"Dan, thank you. This has been quite a few days."

"It has. In a day or so the Task Force will want you in for a debrief. We do thank you."

"Dan?" I asked. "Who are you really?"

"Well, only part of the guy you think I am. I fought under Rex Young in Nam. His life and his death changed me. Looking after Bo changed me. A few years after serving in Southeast Asia, I did a real self-evaluation. Things changed for me. I still struggle with some things mostly from the past, but I am a good cop and I do my job. Everything you have seen has been my job."

"We are just part of your business, right? None of it is personal, right?" I asked.

"It's a little personal, of course. We have known each other a long time. Not all of it has been roses. But this operation has brought my past and my present together. As a result, I don't think you are the total douchebag I once thought." He did smile.

"Nor are you," I had to admit.

249

He said, "One day at a time. I did tell Bo that if he ever hassled you again, I'd arrest him myself. He's still my brother."

"Of course."

Chapter 73
The Broader Scope of Things

The next couple of weeks were a blur. Christmas was coming and Odessa, as always, celebrated it publicly and energetically. I know it's curious to see representations of snow and fir trees in a desert but with the lights downtown and in various neighborhoods, it is easy to get into a certain happy mood during a West Texas Christmas. With all this and moving back into our jobs, JayJay and I settled once again into a semi-regular routine. We did meet the Task Force and we did agree not to reveal any "sources or methods" about how it operated. To me that mostly meant not telling anyone about Dan Gladstone's real life or real persona. It was important for folks to see him as a disgruntled cop and fuck up. We still did not know for sure which one of the three suspects killed Freddie, but my best estimate was Aaron somehow acted impulsively that fateful night. Her death led to a chain reaction that led to a reckoning that now seemed both inevitable and yet unpredictable.

I know you're wondering about that the home on Lake Brownwood. It is in Dan's name, but it does not belong to him and it is not luxurious. It's a meeting place where the War on Drugs higher ups meet to plan operations outside the public glare. It is also used as a temporary way station for snitches and victims when necessary. What does Bo know? He knows his brother has "come to Jesus" and he hopes Bo will work harder to be a better person. Other than that Bo has no idea what Dan works on every day and, being

Bo, he is not at all curious about it. Right now he just hopes to escape a big fine or worse in his insurance business. I don't give a rat's ass.

Then there is Bill O'Toole. We actually don't know exactly what happened to Bill but perhaps someday we will find out. We know that he was arrested, but there has been no newspaper or TV coverage. JayJay and I have visions of the Task Force "turning him" to work for them. Do we watch too many movies? Will we learn more sometime later? Will we ever again cross paths with him? I hope to God not.

We are back on Santa Rita Dr. I am back at work. We paid Willie for his time and added a $1,000 bonus. Jack took great care of Jencks and Associates while I was MIA and he regrets not playing a bigger role during the endgame. M. A. is proud of her role and Beth is not being told anything. None of them knows the whole story. I hope everyone is OK with having me around the office again. JayJay and I have not stopped talking about how clever she was or how brave we both were to trust the Odessa Police Department and do the Plan B, decoy gambit. It worked but JayJay summed it all up at the end of a long night just the day before New Year's Eve.

"You know, I thought this was our story but, in fact, we were just Rosencrantz and Guildenstern," she said.

"Who?" I asked.

"You know Tom Stoppard's play about two minor characters in Hamlet who think the play is about them?"

"I must have missed class that day," I suggested.

"It's human nature to think we were the main stars in the story, but it was much bigger and much more complicated than we ever dreamed."

"Sure, that's true. But at least we came out the other side alive and well," I said

JayJay concluded, "Right and nothing like that will probably ever happen to us again."

"That's for sure. My sleuthing days are over," I said.

Then the phone rang.

Afterword

This I know for sure: success, growth, and meaning in life come from human connections that one must always cultivate.

As an only child I often felt alone and adrift. My parents, Depression Children, from Southern Illinois, lived in fear and isolation at all times. They feared the return of economic hard times; they feared big cities and Big Government, and they feared people who did not look like them, white, rural, and ill-educated. To a child, these fears came as received wisdom rather than prejudice or a limited worldview. Like all parents, they thought they understood the world and they set out to educate me through language and behavior. Unfortunately, their language reflected bigotry and my behavior was sometimes subject to harsh punishment or frequent belittling. My mother came not to trust the man she married, so I learned that men were no good and, of course, I was a little man. My father thought to be a man required independence and complete self-absorption. Both came from the bottom of a liquor bottle. As a child, I just wanted to play, to have friends, and to enjoy people around me, but we moved from Illinois to Missouri to Louisiana to California to Texas all before I turned eight years old. I thought I could simply not make friends because my mother called me by a girl's name, Shelly.

Growing up in deep West Texas, I learned that most of the people in that city, the fastest growing town in

America in the 50s, came from somewhere else and most, but not all, shared my parents' attitudes and fears. The town was rabidly conservative, but it was diverse. I met Jewish people, Hispanic people, kids from big cities, and I met and interacted with African-Americans who worked at my dad's car wash. I now consider it fortunate that I began working at the car wash at eight years old (to learn the value of a dollar, you understand). At the car wash, the black folks I met became an alternative universe to the other one around me. They were smart, funny, good-hearted, and most of all human in their good and bad traits. I simply could not generalize about them like the ones I often heard from my parents and friends. Civil rights to me became human rights. I was 10 at the time.

Odessa's then excellent schools afforded opportunities to learn formally and to play sports. The latter was no small matter since Texas is famous for football and the teams from Odessa then and in the immediate future were among the greatest in the nation. My high school, Odessa Permian, became a symbol of sports' obsession in America through a book, a movie, and a TV show, Friday Night Lights. I determined in the fifth grade to become a football player to overcome my fears and to prove myself worthy as a man. The man I wanted to impress most, my father, chose not to come to my games, but other connections I made with teammates and coaches helped me learn to set goals, work hard, and perform within a group to achieve excellence. My last coach also saw a spark of intelligence in me, so he gave me the Oxford History of the English Language as a graduation gift. I also received the Outstanding Senior Man Award as I graduated high school, but it made little difference to me then because just a year before one of my most important human connections, my first cousin, Betty Williams, was murdered. I was in a fog for more than a year after that.

Betty was a year older than I. She shared my Southern Illinois roots and the influences of a family rooted in evangelicalism, rural values, and male dominance. Betty and I did not grow up together, but she moved to Odessa at 12 when I was 11. She immediately became my most important connection. She was fast becoming an actor, an irrepressible personality, and a rebel. Our long talks about family, politics, race, relationships, and, most of all, dreams about escaping Odessa helped me understand the world and myself in it. She was my mentor. She was also an emerging Hippie but, in her senior year, she was killed. I have written of the details of all this in a book, but in the trial of the boy who killed her, she was painted as an evil temptress and he was cast as the victim. Nothing has ever rocked my world as much as her loss and that trial.

Directly as a result of that event I also met a girl who became my wife to this day. At ages 19 and 18 we married in part to save each other and to create a life based on love and equality rather than fear and ignorance. We paid our own ways through college, got scholarships for me to train as an educator, and worked together to get her through college 14 years later. She became a civil servant in the Social Security Administration. Our two children were never taught fear and hatred.

These events and lessons made me into a professor. I wanted to help young people not only learn from lectures and books but to become part of something bigger whether it was a college, a Model UN Team, a Leadership Program or global citizenship. I wanted to be there for them as an educator, a mentor, and a window to a possible future. I took them to Russia, China, New York, Germany, and Washington, DC. When they lost their parents' favor for being gay, switching majors, or choosing the wrong political party, I was there to listen. I served in the government 4 times but always returned to college teaching to share my insights with students. Later, I began writing a series of books to let others know that if they wish to base their lives on love and understanding, they are not in fact alone.

Friends and former students: You may think you are in this book, but you are not. This is a work of fiction and all the characters are fictional mash-ups of people in the various places I have lived in the past seventy years. Covey and I may share some traits, like a love of "talking in movies," but the differences are way more important than the similarities. I have not lived in Odessa, Texas for fifty-five years and my short visits there since have been more for research on another book than in taking measure of the politics or race relations of the town. I simply assume a few things—that folks are nice, that some racism still exists, that the wind still blows—but as JayJay and Covey know, assumptions can mislead. I know absolutely nothing about how the Drug War has played out there and I know less about the people on the south side. I did know at one time about south Odessa and I did learn to dance there, but that was a long time ago in a galaxy far away. Once again, this book is fiction.

A word about Austin College. The three professors and the College President Covey mentions are real. So is the town lawyer, but I never worked for him. They were friends and colleagues of mine for four decades. I was never a student there and though Luckett Hall did at one time exist, I do not recall ever going in the place. I made it all up. Sure, some may assert that Luckett was a sort of "Animal House," but I think every college in every state has a place they call Animal House and in truth things are tamer in reality.

I started thinking about this book in 2008 after an Odessa Permian reunion, the last one I will ever attend. I did play football there back in the early sixties and I was also on many kick-off units. My record for tackles on that special team assignment was not quite as good as Covey's but then I did not quit my senior year. I played and in fact started at right guard. I forged many friendships on that team and at that school. Most of them have melted away over time, but thanks to Facebook, not all of them. To be pointed, however, the 2008 reunion, the presidential elections that followed, and the various interactions with classmates since have informed much of the content of this book. I say this with some regret, but the 2016 election showed us in stark relief the deep divisions and differing worldviews permeating American society. I, for one, do not think of the 50s and 60s as Happy Days and I do not consider what has happened the last forty years in the U.S. to be a decline. I always see more social inclusion and more racial justice as a struggle for the "more perfect union." Like I say, different worldviews.

I do know this about Permian and about Odessa. In 1961, I met my Bonnie J. there. Bonnie Janell Hollis was her name then. For the past 53 years, she has been better known as Janell Williams and she is every bit as beautiful, smart, and sassy as JayJay. With all the chaos in the world since the sixties, she has been the center of my universe and the foundation of my life. For my second book in a row, she has also been my muse.

That said, I dedicate this book to Quincy Dixon Hunter-Williams and Dylan Lorraine Collins. Pops loves telling you "Deputy Dan" stories, so he decided to write a grown-up version that you can read later in your life. That way you can know how much you are loved and how we can always be together.